MURDER ON MAGAZINE

A SKIP LANGDON MYSTERY

JULIE SMITH

BOOKSBNIMBLE

booksBnimble Publishing
New Orleans, La.

Murder on Magazine

Copyright 2018 by Julie Smith

Print ISBN: 978-0-9998131-0-2
eBook ISBN: 978-0-9973630-9-8

First booksBnimble Publishing electronic publication: 2018

www.booksbnimble.com

All the characters and events in this story are fictitious.

CONTENTS

To Lee, as always, and also to Rambla's best friends who aren't us — Janet and Steve Haedicke

Acknowledgments

Many thanks to Steve Nilles, who had the idea and also who made it happen! Thanks also to Mittie Staininger, who helped, and to Nevada Barr for Thursdays, among many other things, some of them art, some of them help (editorial and otherwise), a lot of them laughs.

And thanks to Covenant House for the amazing work they do.

1

"Short walk to Magazine," say the real estate ads, clueing you in that the neighborhood is ruined. At least it is if you liked it the old way, with its funky little shotguns — many in disrepair but cute as Bahamian bungalows — going on for blocks at a stretch, each eccentrically landscaped in the style of the residents and painted any kind of way. Now they were being bought up by developers and gutted, the doubles turned into singles, which didn't show from the outside, but in way too many cases camelbacks or even undisguised second stories were crammed onto them. They just didn't look right on those small lots.

But of course that was only true in some Uptown neighborhoods, not the whole length of Magazine, the best shopping street in New Orleans — and possibly America. The liveliest part of Magazine, with all its shops and restaurants, goes on for almost three and a half miles. It's no Worth Avenue or Rodeo Drive, but a whole different animal, a destination amusement in itself if you just want to walk and window-shop, maybe stop for a latte or po'boy. It used to be known for junk shops and good deals, and there are still a few second-hand stores. But most good deals have gone the way of such New Orleans institutions as K&B and Maison Blanche. Upscale antique stores still abound, along with every kind of other kind of store or service you can imagine. If you need something, you can flat-out find it on Magazine.

On a random morning, you can get your hair done and your facial fuzz removed, your cat vaccinated and your laptop fixed, and then go for a pizza or anything else you can dream up — sushi, Ethiopian, Caribbean tapas, upscale po' boys, brunch at all hours, even old school neighborhood cooking at Joey K's. After lunch, you could purchase some fancy athletic gear at any of a number of chic boutiques and pop over to Cycle Bar to work off the indulgent lunch. By then it might be time for an afternoon refreshment, maybe at the Bulldog, where you could watch the sporting event of the day. And after that, the amusements could go on into the evening and, frankly, through the night until you found yourself on a barstool at Miss Mae's at 6 a.m.

With still a lot more of Magazine to see.

EXACTLY WHAT SHE was seeing now — aside from a crime scene on Magazine Street — Sergeant Skip Langdon wasn't sure. She'd found herself following a couple of district officers through a bright magenta door — a trickle of blood flowing underneath it — between a store that sold nothing but fancy umbrellas and another that featured high-end party underwear. At least that was what Skip called it. With all that scratchy lace and those awkward straps, you couldn't wear it much longer than it would take your sweetie to rip it off — and there went a few hundred bucks.

The magenta place had no sign. Was it connected to the underwear store? The door opened to a broad staircase, the stairs and railing painted the same jaunty color, although it was currently stained with blackish blood and marred by the dead body of a man more or less sitting, as if placed there, on one of the steps.

On another step, near the bottom and upside down, lay a heavy-looking green Buddha — the sort you might put in the garden or on a mantel — about a foot high, and chipped on top of the head, as if it had suffered a calamitous trip down those roseate stairs. Sure enough, she saw a large-ish green chip on a stair further up. The Buddha was dark with blood and so were a few of the steps in its path, but she didn't see a lot of blood on the victim. She wasn't going to examine him — that was for the coroner — but the officers who'd answered the call must have gotten up fairly close.

"Did you guys touch him?" she asked.

"I did," said the white one, Officer Stewart by his nametag. "I don't know why. He looks about forty-eight hours dead. Maybe less — there's still a little rigor."

He was probably right. The dead man was turning green, which happens after about a day and a half, and his tongue protruded. Fortunately, it was early January, so the smell wasn't overwhelming. The call had come from neighbors who noticed blood had leaked under the door.

"Blood on him?" Skip asked.

Stewart indicated the man's face. "Well he kind of looks like he's been in a fight, but I didn't see any knife or gunshot wounds."

A fight. Yes. That was what it looked like. But how did the man die?

"Did you guys secure the scene?"

Wilkinson, the black one, nodded. "Yeah. Pretty weird up there."

She ought to wait for the coroner to remove the body. But that could take a while and who knew what these guys had missed?

On the other hand, who was she kidding? She was itching to get up there, to get started on this thing. The uniforms had gone up without tracking blood — so could she. She had booties. Pulling them on, she said, "You guys wait here. I'm going up."

At the top of the stairs was a hall, maybe ten feet wide, with Indian style art on the walls and a small table with a few imported items marked for sale — bracelets, earrings, a few scarves. But the place didn't look like a store.

Two open doors led into two connecting empty rooms, pocket doors between them open so they flowed into one long room decorated only with mirrors above two mantels. On one of the mantels sat a complacent green Buddha exactly like his twin downstairs.

The two rooms opened onto a third, also with open pocket doors. This one was furnished, though. Skip's first impression was of a rumpled bed and black-painted writing on the wall. She barely noticed the other furniture. She was riveted by the wall, unbelieving: "Blackass bitch spicaninny snigger mexcrement batman diaperhead BMO."

Oh, man!

She'd seen something like this before, about a month earlier, or pictures of it. Maybe the moon's full — I wonder if the guy's a werewolf, she thought inanely.

The guy. She knew it was the same guy. Serial killer was her first heart-pounding fear. But there hadn't been a body the first time — the victim had narrowly escaped. She was quite literally a blackass bitch — a female pit bull — very messed up. Skip shuddered.

She glanced around the room, feeling her heart race, sweat popping out, the bottom falling out of her stomach. This was no ordinary homicide, if there was such a thing. But what was it? Some kind of hate crime? Wasn't murder always a hate crime? And certainly serial murder! WTF, she thought.

On the floor beside a chair were a pair of zip-tie handcuffs, and a pair of metal ones were attached to the headboard of the bed.

Fighting the ants in her pants, the crazy desire to just do something — anything — she kept up her inspection.

Behind this bedroom was another large room with a fireplace, done up as a living room with a slightly Indian feel, which wasn't hard these days, even in New Orleans, due to the availability of Indian imports. Behind that was a kitchen with a door to the outside — pretty odd for a second floor. Testing, Skip saw that it opened onto an enclosed upstairs porch decked with potted plants, many of them blooming, and furnished with a long picnic table. The whole structure was strung with tiny decorative lights, with more lights wrapped round the bigger plants. Skip found it jaw-dropping. Whoever lived here — or had lived here — had very nice taste, she decided.

But what was up with those two empty rooms? She walked into the first, which was furnished with only the mirror and the Buddha. The second opened onto a balcony overlooking Magazine Street and there was another door here, near the balcony on the right. Evidently the room it opened onto overhung the staircase. Flinging open the shutters, she saw that the balcony was also furnished nicely —

lights and plants here too, with a couple of bistro tables and chairs.

The mysterious door led to the most prosaic of spaces — a walk-in closet, but one that provided the key to the whole set up. Built-in shelves held yoga mats, blankets, and blocks, and there was a small desk and cashbox where, evidently, yogis attended to the mundane. So the apartment must be a live-work space, the work part being a yoga studio. Very clever use of space, Skip thought, but wondered why there was no outside sign to identify it.

Pulling on vinyl gloves, she rifled the desk. Sure enough, it yielded Buddhist and Hindu texts, probably used for readings in class, some checkbooks, and what looked like students' payments. Thank the Buddhist gods (if there were any), there were also some magenta business cards. They gave the address of the building, a phone number, and the studio's apparent name: Namaste Bitch.

Namaste Bitch?

Was that anything like "blackass bitch"?

2

W

as the guy on the stairs the Namaste Bitch? And maybe the blackass bitch as well? Anyone could be a bitch, she supposed, but could this guy be considered black? People tend to lose their looks in death, but she'd imagined him Latino. He was short and lithe, a very passable yogi build.

Could have been playing sex games with a partner and things got out of hand, but...a very disturbed partner, Skip thought. The case of the injured dog (whom the whole city had come to know as Sheba), had been investigated by the ASPCA, but pictures of the animal and the spray-painted wall behind it had been the subject of much speculation in Homicide, none of it very optimistic. Serial killers nearly always started with animals — and also there was that wall of hate. It sure looked like someone was practicing.

Maybe the guy who lived here — the yogi — had picked up his killer in a bar. She wondered if the hate-wall had been applied pre- or post-mortem.

Hearing a commotion below, she ducked out in the small hall to salute the techs and coroner's investigators, who were just now trooping in. "Get out of my crime scene!" someone yelled up at her, but she didn't. She went out on the balcony and dialed the number on the card, wondering if it would ring somewhere in the studio, maybe in the dead man's pocket. She half-expected one of her colleagues to pick up.

But instead a female voice said in a businesslike way, "Namaste Bitch," much in the same tone a legal secretary might intone, "Langdon, Stein, and Ritter."

Skip improvised. "Hi, are you a yoga studio?"

"Yes, but I'm sorry to say we're closed for the next week and a half. Classes start again Monday after next."

"Are you the owner?"

"Mr. Dustin De Blanc is the owner, but he's currently unavailable. May I help you with something?"

"Dustin De Blanc. That has quite a ring to it."

Skip wasn't really aware she'd spoken aloud, but the woman said, "Yes. That's why we named him that."

Oh, damn you, Buddhist gods! If you exist. His MOTHER?

She proceeded cautiously. "When will Mr. De Blanc be in?"

"He's out of town for the week, I'm afraid, but I can help with whatever you need."

"May I ask where your studio is located?"

Mrs. De Blanc gave the address of the building Skip was standing in.

"Mrs. De Blanc, this is Sergeant Skip Langdon of the New Orleans Police Department. I wonder if you could give me a number where I can reach him?"

"The police? Why do the police need him? Please tell me the building didn't burn down! I knew there was a gas leak in there — he's had it tested about a hundred times, but I can smell it every time I get in savasana."

"No, the building's fine, but we need to speak with your son. Can you give me his cell phone number?"

"This is his cell phone. I told you — he's unavailable. Can you please tell me what the emergency is?"

Skip didn't at all like the sound of that. Who gives their cell phone to their mother? Or anyone. Maybe this wasn't his mother. "We need to reach him, ma'am. Can you help me out?"

Mama sighed, but sounded a little put out. "Well, it's no secret. He's on a retreat in Texas."

"What kind of retreat?"

"The kind where they don't talk for ten days. Meditation only. And you come back a better person." She giggled. "It's never worked before, but you never know."

"I see. May I have the number of the retreat?"

"Okay, Sergeant, I've about had it! You haven't answered a single one of my questions and I've answered all of yours. What's this all about?"

"Tell me, does anyone else live at the studio? Or only your son?"

"Oh, goddammit, so that's it! That goddam bastard landlord's behind this, isn't he? It's that motherfreakin' Sanford bastard, excuse me very much." And with that she hung up, leaving Skip grinning. Why would anyone curse out a police officer, apologize for it, and then hang up — in that order? Skip didn't care. If that was Dustin De Blanc on those stairs, it bought her a little time before she had to break the news to his devoted mom and answering service.

She descended to talk to the crime scene team. Permelia Read, a young eager beaver with a near-genius IQ and the willowy body of a fashion model, was just coming up the stairs. "Hey, Skip. How's it going?" She had her honey-blonde hair up in one of those plastic clamps with teeth.

"To quote the district guys, it's pretty weird up there."

"Yeah, I heard."

"Hey, did his pockets turn up anything? ID? Cell phone? Stolen diamonds?"

Read shrugged. "Couple Penny Blacks, that was it." She and Read had an ongoing joke about the valuable things corpses never had on them. But Skip was disappointed.

"The perp must have emptied his pockets before he took off," Skip said. "You know, there's something weird, though. The door was locked when the district guys got here. And this just doesn't look like a suicide. Somebody else was here, for sure. I mean, with that heavy bust thing down there and all the blood... and the fact that the victim isn't bloody. He's got a closed head wound, though. Could have been hit with that thing."

"Maybe he was hit while coming down the stairs. Maybe the two of them fought, the victim drew blood, and the perp clobbered him. The perp could have left him alive and then the victim locked the door and climbed back up, but only made it a few steps."

"How about his pockets being empty?"

"Well, if he lives here, they might be, right? If you're not going out, you don't need anything. Think he's the owner?"

"Tenant. But I don't know. I talked to his mother — meaning the tenant's mother; I found his card upstairs — and she said he's on a religious retreat. But I gather there's some kind of dispute with the landlord. Maybe that's who killed him."

"Wouldn't that be easy!"

"Anybody wants me, I'm canvassing."

Since nobody had reported hearing a fight, Skip didn't have a lot of hope that someone had seen the killer leave, but she might do better after the time of death was established. This was a heavily commercial neighborhood, with two restaurants very close, which meant wait staff on smoke breaks. So there were things to be learned.

She started with the next door neighbors, but the clerk in the umbrella store, the one who'd seen the blood, was new and didn't know even know there was a yoga studio next door, much less who lived upstairs. "Try next door," she said, "Bette knows everything."

Next door was the kind of store that was too upscale to be quite a junk store and yet carried merchandise too new to be vintage. In other words, you could get home furnishings here, but they'd probably be overpriced and poor quality. "I'm looking for Bette," she announced to a youngish saleslady, who didn't have time to answer.

"You found her, dawlin'," said a disembodied voice.

Bette, it seemed, was out of sight, adjusting something behind a counter, but when she stood up, she was still pretty much out of sight. She must have been about four-feet-eleven, so skinny you could see most of her veins, in her seventies, short hair, glasses, and enough attitude for three people twice her size. "What can I do you for?"

Skip showed her badge and said her rank, which was fairly new. She still got a kick out of saying "sergeant."

"I'm wondering if you know anything about the yoga studio," she began, not wanting to say its name.

"Namaste Bitch?" Bette said. "Oh, sure. I do restorative at least once a week and morning flow when I can. Been knowin' Dustin ever since he moved in. Know his mama too, and everybody from Vinyasa and Vino — I go just for the vino, still working during the class. What's going on over there today?"

"You mean you didn't hear?" Skip knew Bette had to know. She was the kind of woman who knew everything in her neighborhood.

"I heard Emaline next door saw blood under the door and when the first cops came, they found somebody dead. Who was it?"

"A man, short — about five eight maybe — and fairly dark. Maybe not African-American, but could be Latino. Dustin's French, right?"

"Well, that ain't Dustin, I can damn well tell ya that. He's six feet if he's an inch. And anyway, he's on the shelf."

"On the shelf?" Inwardly she was thinking, Thank you, Buddha gods. No breaking bad news to the grieving mom!

"The shelf's what he calls it when he goes off to one of those meditation retreats."

"Any idea who the dead guy might be? Does Dustin have a roommate or anything?"

"No, no roommate. Hey, I'll look at him if he's still there." She shrugged her birdlike shoulders. "Maybe he's a student. Or somebody from the 'hood."

"I'd appreciate that." Works for everybody, Skip thought. Bette satisfies her curiosity and maybe I get an I.D.

But she didn't get an I.D., just the opinion that the victim "looked like he'd been dead a week and a half." And wasn't Dustin's type.

"Dustin's type? You mean romantic type?"

"Dustin's gay as a blade. But he likes 'em older."

The corpse looked twenty-five or so. "How old is Dustin?"

"Thirty and pretty. A treat for the eyes. He likes what he

calls 'hot daddies'. You know... older than he is."

"I heard he was in some kind of hassle with his landlord. This guy wouldn't be him, right?"

"Oh, hell, no! Robbie Sanford's my landlord too. Owns half the block. He's about my age."

"Guess I better give him a call." Skip asked for his number and continued her canvassing, but Bette proved her best source by far.

Smoking waiters from Juan's Flying Burrito hadn't heard or seen anything, or else were off that day, nor had any of the shopkeepers and clerks. Since most of the buildings on the block were the old Creole style — shops downstairs, living space upstairs — there were other residents besides Dustin, but most weren't home. She was particularly interested in the neighbors across the street, the ones whose balconies and front windows directly faced Dustin's, and indeed she found someone home above another restaurant — Israel Boykin, a young and shaggy stoner, if the smell was any clue.

He wouldn't let Skip in, but he did agree to have a conversation from his balcony in a pair of sweatpants and no shirt. Reflecting on the general indignity of the job, she yelled up at him, pointing across the street. "You know your neighbor, Dustin De Blanc?"

"The yoga guy? He's dead, right? I saw 'em take him away."

Oh, hell, this wasn't going well — she hadn't expected him to go there. "Look, this isn't working. Can you just come down?"

"Whathehell, you only asked me one thing — already it isn't working?"

"Israel, do you really want the whole neighborhood to overhear our conversation?"

He shrugged. "Izzy. Who cares?"

"Hey, is that pot I smell? It's still illegal, you know." Everyone knew the New Orleans police usually let it go.

"Naaah. Definitely not pot," he said, but she thought he was a little chastened.

"You've got ninety seconds to put on a shirt and get down here," she hollered in as mean a voice as she could muster, and he disappeared. That was better. It was humiliating to have a cop yelling orders at you.

When he arrived on the sidewalk, he'd not only suited up like a gentleman (added sweatshirt and sneakers), but tamed his curls. Skip grinned. "I must have really scared you."

"Naaah. It was time I got up anyway." He gave her a too-careful onceover. "How tall are you?"

"Five feet twelve, if it's any of your business."

He did it again. "You could be attractive, you know that? How much do you weigh?"

"What are you, an out-of-work hairdresser?"

"Personal trainer." He seemed offended. "And definitely not out of work. I take clients on my own time."

"Well, I hope your clients don't know how much you smoke. What's the story on your neighbor?"

"Hey, I don't even know him. I just like to look in the window and watch the pretty ladies turn into pretzels. Not much going on lately, though."

"Bad week for voyeurism — he cancelled classes this week. See anyone else over there the last few days?"

He shrugged. "I don't think so, but I don't even notice any more, they come and go so often. Sometimes groups of six or eight... You never know who's gonna be there."

"You mean people staying overnight? Like... mini yoga retreats, maybe?"

"Naaah. I don't think the dead guy really lives there. I think it's an Airbnb joint."

"Why do you think that?"

"It turns over a lot, even on weekdays. Random people sit on the balcony at night and talk too loud. Know what I mean?"

Skip definitely did. After years living in the French Quarter, she couldn't count the times she'd been awakened by someone's early-morning balcony revels. Tourists, exhilarated by the 24-hour culture, came home too wound up to sleep and too drunk to keep quiet, and went out on the balcony for another round.

"How about the last few days?"

Izzy plucked at his moustache, an evil glint in his eye. "Quiet as a tomb. Oops. Should I not have said that?"

"Cops," she said, "are not immune to black humor." It wasn't actually funny, but she might need this guy later.

"You're ok, Sergeant. Call me if you ever want to buff up."

She handed him her card. "You call me if you think of anything that might help."

Next on the agenda was Robbie Sanford, the guy who owned half the block. He undoubtedly had a key. So could he be the murderer and wall-writer? Doubtful, she thought — Dustin probably wouldn't have mentioned he was going to be away. Still, she thought it best to see him in person. She phoned, got an address, and found herself headed for Metairie, where Sanford lived in a '50s ranch-style house that to Skip's mind wasn't nearly as nice as Dustin's live-work space.

He met Skip at the door with a walker. "Just had knee surgery."

"You need to sit down right now, too," said a bustling woman in the background who was undoubtedly Mrs.

Sanford and who bore an uncanny resemblance to Bette from the semi-vintage store. Not a sister resemblance, just a tribal one — small, skinny, and acerbic, like so many Louisiana women.

Sanford himself was pretty nondescript, with brown thinning hair worn too long and a pointy chin.

"I have some upsetting news, I'm afraid," Skip said, "Someone's died in one of your apartments on Magazine St. — the yoga studio."

Sanford looked utterly at sea. Finally, he said, "Yoga studio?"

"Namaste Bitch," she said and gave the address.

"Excuse me?"

"That's what he calls it — your tenant."

"Dustin. Nice young man. Oh, lord, don't tell me Dustin's dead! What was it? A drug overdose?"

"How tall would you say Dustin is?"

"Oh, at least six feet. Tall handsome Cajun-looking guy. You know, dark hair and eyes — very French looking."

Skip had no idea what it meant to look French — or anything else, any more. "The dead man's about five-eight," she said. "Tell me, is Dustin living there?"

"If he isn't, I'd sure as hell like to know who is. He's running a yoga studio out of that place?"

"Well... that might not be the only thing. He seems to be renting it out to..."

"Oh, hell no, he'd better not be! You mean he's turned that apartment into a short-term rental unit? He's gonna wish he was dead, I'm gonna tell you that, in the event he turns out not to be." He stopped in mid-sentence. "Hey! If he's not dead, where is he? Why aren't you asking him this stuff?"

"He's taken a vow of silence," Skip said.

3

For awhile, the Homicide Unit had been de-centralized, with the detectives working out of district stations, but it was now back under one roof, safe at Headquarters. After a stint in District Three, Skip was back on S. Broad with a couple of her favorites, Sergeant Adam Abasolo and Sylvia Cappello, now commander of the unit.

If truth be told, Abasolo was probably the officer she most liked to work with in the entire department. Aside from being drop-dead handsome (a condition she'd long since stopped being awed by), he was a great cop and an even better friend. He was waiting for her now, something steamy and enticing in his hand. "Got you a cuppa joe."

But not your average cuppa joe — a skinny vanilla latte, and how many colleagues were that thoughtful? This wasn't always her usual, only when she wanted to indulge, which he very well knew. "You must want something."

"How could you even go there? I heard you and Steve are having a crisis — just wanted you to know I'm there for you."

"What? Who told you that?"

He shrugged. "Cindy Lou. Who else?" The department psychologist and one of Skip's best friends. Evidently she'd been talking out of school. Skip wondered if this meant Abasolo was getting any closer to asking her out — he had a long-term crush on the psychologist, but never seemed to get up the nerve to make his move. Which might be just as well for his mental health, in Skip's opinion. Cindy Lou had a history with men.

"Well, thanks for the thought. So what do you want?"

He gave her his patented Italian movie star grin. "Okay, okay, you're too smart for me." And then a quick point down the hall. "The commander wants to be briefed. Can I sit in?"

"Oh, you heard about the case. What was it you liked?"

He shook his head, as if contemplating something plain wrong. "The wall writing. This could be a serial killer. Could be a task force."

"If you're volunteering, you could have saved your latte money — you'd be my first pick anyhow. You know that."

He laughed. "You're pretty arrogant. What makes you think you're going to get to lead it?"

"Try and take it from me," she said and pulled out her phone. She placed a call to Namaste Bitch, aka Dustin De Blanc's mom, and told her just enough to get the name of The Lotus Ranch, just outside Houston. It was uphill work, but the mellow person who answered the phone was finally made to understand that murder trumped mindfulness, at least in the short run. Skip opted to have Dustin call her back rather than be summoned now, perhaps in the middle of a life-changing insight. Her main mission was accomplished — she'd learned Dustin was definitely at The Lotus Ranch and had been for the last four days.

When Permelia Reed from the Crime Scene team arrived, Skip and Abasolo joined her in Cappello's office.

The commander said, "Langdon, I hear it's a nasty one."

"Definitely not your run-of–the-mill homicide. Remember Sheba?"

"Of course." Sheba was kind of a local phenomenon. She was the dog the whole city knew about — the pit bull who'd suffered horrible injuries a month ago when a passerby came upon an unknown man attacking her. The man ran, the rescuer adopted the dog, whom he named Sheba, and both became local heroes. Skip produced a picture of the fence behind which the pooch had been found.

Everyone passed it around and shook their heads. Everyone remembered. Everyone had been alarmed when it happened. Skip said, "Could be our worst fears were justi-fied. Especially since this was December 2."

It was now January 4, and the murder — if it was one — could easily have been committed on January 2. Most likely was, marking the beginning of a pattern.

"Well, let's not panic yet," Read said. "because the good news is, the stiff's probably our guy. Pretty sure there was a woman there that night. We found some blood on the bed and also some long curly hair, pink on the ends — meaning the last few inches."

"Oh," Skip said. "Really long hair."

"What do you call that?" asked the commander. "There's a name for that. I'm thinking of getting it."

"You're thinking of getting what?" asked Read.

"That color on the end thing. What do you call it?"

"It's got a name?" Abasolo was clearly impatient, but the commander was making Skip grin. How many times had she sat in meetings while men digressed onto football scores or — worse — the comparative attractiveness of the women involved in a case? This was kind of refreshing.

"Well, don't get pink," Read said. "You should go for blue. It would totally go with the uniform."

"OK," said Skip. "So how about this? Either the woman or the perp rents the apartment on Airbnb, they either know each other or don't, they go there for sex, he writes on the wall, she spooks, and they fight. Hence the blood on the Buddha. Was the blood on the bed the same type?"

Read nodded. "B positive. But if she attacked the guy with the Buddha, why isn't it his blood? And it isn't. He's O positive."

"All right," Abasolo said. "Maybe she doesn't spook — maybe he tries to kill her. Hey, I've got it — she does spook, and gets up and runs. And then he attacks with the Buddha."

"But then she somehow manages to kill him?" Skip said. "Damn! Sure wish we had the autopsy report."

"If she got just one good blow in, that could have done it," the commander said. "Or he could have fallen on the stairs and hit his head. Boom! Serial killer hopes dashed."

Skip snickered. She really had no idea whether the commander was making a joke. Cappello was very literal minded, so probably not, but it still struck her funny.

Cappello gave her a look.

Skip pulled herself together. "But the door was locked. How does the woman leave?"

Abasolo shrugged. "Maybe she had her own key."

"Doubtful," Skip said, "unless they were married, and I think we can rule that out. The key was on the bedside table, but the door locks with a deadbolt. So maybe he regained consciousness and locked it himself — didn't want to see that blackass bitch again! By the way, the epithets on the wall referred to at least three different ethnic groups, so he didn't like anybody but white people, I guess. But I'm digressing. Either he locked it himself or she locked it and left another way."

"What other way?" asked the commander.

"There are actually two other ways out — she could have climbed over the front balcony and slid down a pole. She'd risk being seen, but there's a back deck kind of thing. I wonder if she could have gone that way?"

"I believe I can help you there," Read said. "There was blood on one of the poles that hold that thing up, and some broken plants at the bottom. She could have crawled over the wall, slid down the pole, and landed in them."

"Okay, then," said Abasolo. "Locked room mystery solved."

The commander said, "Any idea who the victim was?"

Read shook her head: "No ID, no cell phone, no money, no nothing. We'll have to try for dental records. Maybe fingerprints, but he was young. There might not be any on file."

Skip said, "Can you get someone working on surveillance tape?"

"I'm kind of short-handed. Fazzio's out this week. Let's see." She consulted a roster.

"How about one of those uniforms — Stewart, maybe."

"Yeah, good. They're already invested." Evidently deciding the meeting was over, the commander summed it up. "All right then, our best theory is that the victim was the perv who wrote on the wall, right? And he had a fatal fight with his intended victim, an injured pink-haired woman, for whom we are now looking. Everyone in agreement?"

Everyone nodded.

"So no task force," Skip said to Abasolo as they walked back down the hall. "Are you disappointed?"

Abasolo looked uncomfortable. "I don't know. I've got a bad feeling. Maybe we'll know more when we get an ID on the victim." Skip picked up her keys. "Hey, where you going?"

"Quick lunch break. Gotta pick up Rambla from doggie day care. Steve'll be home by now."

"Well, give him my best. And tell him I'll kill him if he wins this fight."

Skip laughed. "It's not a fight."

SKIP AND STEVE STEINMAN, her long-term love, had had their ups and downs, but for a long time now they'd been happily cohabiting in Steve's Bywater cottage, which he'd purchased as a sign of his intention to become a New Orleanian. As a filmmaker and Californian, it was quite a commitment.

For a long time, all was not only fine, but became much better than they'd ever hoped as Louisiana's film industry grew, built upon tax credits that made it an attractive place to make a movie. And then the legislature cut the credits — it seemed they were a great benefit to the industry, but not so much to the state.

By that time, Skip and Steve were used to their lovely dual incomes. So now the question was, should Steve relocate to California? And should Skip?

But it wasn't a fight, it was just a discussion — at least at this point. Skip sighed, not wanting to think about it as she drove to her erstwhile home in the French Quarter to get their dog.

Going all soft as she thought of Rambla, it occurred to her that they'd built quite a comfortable life for themselves since what she now thought of as The Siege.

For years their lives had been haunted by Errol Jacomine, a murderer, kidnapper, and con artist with a remarkable talent for avoiding capture and a pressing need to take Skip out. Several times she'd barely escaped with her life, but their previous dog hadn't. Or Steve's dog, really. Steve had originally meant him for Kenny, the adopted son of their friend, Jimmy Dee Scoggin. But Jimmy Dee's boy friend was allergic to him, and Steve loved the brute.

There was a horrible period after Napoleon was murdered. Really, she could only call it that. Jacomine had ordered a hit on an innocent (although obstreperous) dog. Not only Napoleon's loss, but the whole Jacomine episode was horrible, and more so in the aftermath, kind of like when you stopped banging your head against the wall. Because until they'd gotten free of it, they hadn't let down their guard enough to let themselves think about it. They'd gradually and tentatively restructured their lives, finally getting to a point where it all seemed stable. And then the bottom had fallen out — out of their finances, if not their real life.

But the center and symbol of all the rebuilding remained firmly in place, providing the anchor that reminded them of who they were and what they'd been through — their ever-joyful best friend, the much-loved Rambla, not a German shepherd like Napoleon, nor a lab like... well, frankly... pretty much like Steve himself, but a tricolor Cavalier King Charles spaniel with chestnut eyebrows as expressive as an entire vocabulary. To Skip's mind, the world's most beautiful animal. To Steve's, way too small a pooch. In the abstract.

It took him about thirty seconds to fall in love.

Moving to Steve's house (and buying into it! Now it was their house) was both a delight and a wrench, because so much of her life had revolved around Jimmy Dee's chaotic household. She'd moved into his slave quarters after returning from California, where she'd fled from the suffocating Uptown life she was born into. It was in a period when many of Jimmy Dee's friends had died of AIDS. He was depressed. And Skip was disoriented, felt as if she was on thin ice, back in a city she only half-trusted — afraid of being controlled by her social-climbing family, not having any real friends. She and Jimmy Dee fell upon each other like wanderers on a lonely planet.

When he adopted his late sister's children, Kenny and Sheila, the kids became her family almost as much as his. She was already dating Steve, but he lived in California. As he began spending more time in New Orleans and Jimmy Dee started dating Lane, their social circle became warm, tight, and essential. Now Lane lived in the Big House with Jimmy Dee and Kenny. Sheila, these days — to Uncle Jimmy's enduring pride — was a Tulane law student and had taken over Skip's old apartment. And she had a clever little gig for making extra spending money — doggie day care for Skip and Steve.

She and Rambla were waiting on the curb now, in response to a text from Skip.

Skip hoped to hell no informants, miscreants, or fellow cops observed the scene that followed — replete with hugs, tail-wagging, baby talk ("Was she a good girl? Rambla, were you good for Auntie Sheila?"), kisses, and squeals as Sheila settled Rambla into Skip's car.

Sheila had grown into a tall, stunning, sometime-brunette with a bird tattoo on her right shoulder. Truth be told she was almost as tall as Skip and also curvy. (Although no one ever called Skip curvy. Just "a gorgeous hunk of woman" if it was Steve, and "need to lose weight" if Skip.) But no question, Sheila was curvy. In that lush, Latin Sofia Vergara way. And she'd developed a softness of personality to match, especially where Rambla was concerned.

"Everybody good?" Skip said.

"Oh, wait a second." Sheila retrieved a plate from the stoop. "Uncle Lane made coconut cake."

"You monster — you know I can't resist that." But she took it gladly. "Everyone ok?" she repeated.

"Sure, great. Except that Kenny got another piercing. I thought Uncle Jimmy was going to explode trying to keep quiet about it."

Skip had to laugh. "Well, I hope he succeeded — the last time didn't work all that well. Where'd he get pierced?"

Sheila made a face, "Nose."

"Ha! Well, it beats nipples. I guess."

"Ewwwww."

In response to impatient honking, Skip waved and took off, feeling good. Like she belonged. Now that she'd moved, it was moments like these that glued her world together.

Damn! she thought. Forgot to ask her about that two-color hair thing.

4

———

It was less than a day since Cody killed the man. She didn't feel guilty or anything much, except free. Which should have been a great feeling, but it wasn't as great as she'd hoped, because it seemed so unlikely, so unfamiliar. She couldn't convince herself it really belonged to her.

And she knew it wasn't going to last, because she was going to be arrested soon, or perhaps captured or killed. And so she was afraid too. She was a small potato, more like a pea or a blueberry, and everyone else was gigantic, like AK-47 gigantic, and she'd never won anything before, so why should she win this? This race, or fight or showdown — or whatever it was — for her life. It didn't belong to her any more, but she'd stolen it for the moment, and pretty soon she was going to see again the one person who'd ever really cared about her. If that was all there was, at least there was that.

Nothing could be worse than what she'd left behind.

"Lamar, we almost there?" she asked, knowing she was ridiculous, but unable to help herself.

Her driver laughed — yes, her driver. Because she was paying him, something she'd never done before in her life. She'd never hired someone for anything. Never had a cent to call her own. Never even been taken seriously — everyone else she knew would have just robbed her instead of taking the job. "Shouldn't be more than another thousand miles or so," he said, and she liked that he was joking with her. It made her feel more whole, more like a real person. She didn't know what she was any more.

She'd seen her opportunity coming as soon as she knew they were going to the Sugar Bowl. She'd planned it because it was her one chance, while she was in New Orleans, a place she knew people, could get around in, and maybe could see her Maw-Maw again, but nothing she'd planned had worked out. Nothing.

Well, except one thing. She'd vowed to use violence if she had to, to use any means she could think of. She even had a roofie she'd bartered for; she could have used that if things had gone as she imagined. But no way, no possible way had she imagined the way they did go. She didn't intend to kill anybody.

It was a fairly routine set-up, just with a twist or two. It wasn't a hotel room, it was somebody's house. Or apartment, or something. Odd that it had those two empty rooms, but other than that, it was just a place Miguel had found on Airbnb — a place with a bedroom, living room, and kitchen, like any other apartment. Miguel said the customer was paying for it; the customer had certain things he wanted and he was willing to pay for everything to be just right.

Her babysitter — some guy who worked with Miguel — had taken her inside, and set her up the way the john wanted, in a sort of long T-shirt thing, not fancy lingerie, and in bed, as if she was sleeping. "I'll be right outside," he said. "When the putero leaves, get dressed and come find me." (Not "text me." Miguel's girls were not allowed to have cell phones.)

"Only one customer?" Wouldn't that be great! But she knew it couldn't be right. No way she thought Miguel and his buddy Lloyd had brought her and three other girls all the way to New Orleans just for one customer. But still — with this kind of special treatment, the guy had to be a whale.

"Let me worry about that," the bodyguard said.

She'd actually taken a nap. Actually fallen asleep waiting for the john, and then she'd heard him coming upstairs. It was kind of creepy, like a ghost story. But he was a normal enough looking guy, even kind of familiar. Like she'd seen him before.

"Who the hell are you?" he said.

She sat up and fluffed her hair, trying to look pretty, to get this thing over and done with, the way she'd been taught. "Cody," she said.

"What the fuck is that you're wearing? Why aren't you dressed any better than that?"

Had Miguel made an error? Or was this some kind of role-playing thing? She decided that was it and said, "Darlin', I'll wear anything you like. How about this?"

She flipped the nightshirt over her head, but that seemed to enrage him.

"Put that goddam thing back on."

She obeyed quickly, starting to think the guy was a freak, not wanting to goad him into hitting her. She'd run into one once before — they made it your fault they "had to" hit you.

"Get the hell over here."

She got out of the bed and glided over to him, swinging

her hips, meager as they were, trying to look sexy, get this thing on track.

He pushed her backwards. "Sit in the goddam chair." She landed in it. He grabbed her hand, threaded it through the slats of the chair, snatched up the other, and handcuffed her with those plastic cuff things before she fully understood what was happening. "Ooooh, nice," she said, "You like games?"

She was trying to keep her cool. The rule was no handcuffs, ever, unless specified in advance.

"Watch me, bitch." She looked straight at him as ordered, becoming more and more convinced she knew him. And then it came to her. The guy was famous.

He emptied his pockets on the bedside stand, slowly. He made a show of rolling up his sleeves. He drew a pair of latex gloves from a gym bag, and then something else — a can? Yes, a can of spray paint.

And then he painted the wall. "Blackass bitch", and that was the least of it.

This isn't about me, she thought, panicked. I'm not black. I'm not Mexican. I'm white. He didn't mean me.

But she was dark and she had curly hair. Some of the girls even called her "Tex-Mex", partly because of her cowboy name, but she'd also been sent to customers who requested Latina girls. Even black, once. She didn't really know what she was, but she knew a lot of people thought she wasn't white.

She didn't know what to do.

She finally said, "You disappointed, baby? I could call my friend Terry. She's real blonde with skin like... ummm..." she had an inspiration... "like Snow White. All our friends say she looks like Kristen Stewart. You want me to call Terry for you?"

He said, "Shut up, Monica! This is my fucking show for once. You want me to fuck you, right?" His voice softened. "You know you want me, baby. Come on, tell me you want me..."

Cody didn't know about that "Monica" thing, but she sure understood the rest of the dialogue. "Oh, baby, yeah! I want you," she whispered, and trotted out all the other things she'd been taught as well, until she noticed he'd taken out a pair of real handcuffs and put them in place so he could cuff her to the bed.

She'd been trying to pretend this wasn't happening, that she was going to get out of this without getting beat up, or cut up, or maybe... well, of course she knew the "maybe." She hadn't been a whore for two years without her share of terror, but always in the past, if she kept her cool, she could talk her way out, just until she could yell for Miguel. But tonight there was no way her bodyguard could hear her. Miguel had never left her alone like this. She couldn't imagine what this freak was paying, to make Miguel take a chance like this.

Later she thought it was her rage at him that had probably saved her life.

The freak came up behind her and slashed the plastic cuffs with a knife. Automatically, she rubbed her wrists, not having realized how much they hurt. "Get in bed, bitch."

"Anything for you, baby." She had learned that the more she played along, the more the customers bought her act. She brushed at her hair again, getting it out of her eyes, but also activating her secret weapon — the only weapon she had. She'd never used it before, but she'd never been this freaked out.

It was a near-invisible hairpin, very much like a bobby pin — just a sliding clip made from a bent wire. Only both ends of this one had been sharpened into deadly needles. It could be hidden easily and accessed easily. The only trick was, you had to be quick and you had to be accurate. But she'd spent hours practicing with Miguel and the other girls, with real bobby pins so nobody got hurt. She wasn't confident, but she knew this was her only shot.

She turned towards the freak, smiling. "Kiss me first?" She raised her hand as if to touch the side of his face, perhaps to hug him around the neck, and at the last split-second, drove the pin into his eye.

The other eye dilated as she watched, the black as big as a bumblebee, and the roar that came out of him could have been Simba's. She knew enough to run — that was the second lesson, after "go for the eye". She ran the only way she could, into the two empty rooms, and he was right after her. She needed another weapon, and, true to her Catholic background, prayed for one. For the first time in her life, her prayer was answered. There was only one thing in the first room — a weapon. A great big stone weapon, sitting on top of the mantel. She snatched up the Buddha and ran for the stairs.

He chased her, blood pouring, she could feel him in her wake — no time to just try to beat him down the stairs. She feinted backward, hoping he couldn't see where she was, that the pain was too great to allow a whole lot of thinking and planning. Sure enough, he stepped in front of her. She wanted to try to kick him down the stairs, but wasn't sure she was heavy enough. Instead, she threw the Buddha full into his back, wishing she could have hit his head, but the weapon was too heavy and she was too short.

The Buddha worked, though. Struck in the back, he stumbled and fell backward down the stairs. She picked up the Buddha and threw it after him. Hitting him again, maybe knocking him out, maybe killing him. And then she picked it up again and hit him yet again, raising the thing over her head and bringing it down on his.

When he was still, she ran up the stairs again, already realizing she had to escape on her own. Miguel couldn't help her, and she didn't want that anyway. His hired guy was outside and this whole night was supposed to be about escaping from Miguel, although how it was going to happen she hadn't yet figured out. Killing the customer was a strategy she hadn't thought of.

She remembered something — he'd emptied his pockets upstairs. There had to be money there — and with luck, a phone. Racing back through the house, she found the money and yes! A phone. She stuffed all that and her clothes into the freak's bag, grabbed the bag, finding it unexpectedly heavy, and, thinking maybe she could somehow hide from the babysitter, maybe climb over the balcony, she started to case the apartment.

And then she saw that back door.

At first she didn't believe it. How could there possibly be a back way when she was on the second floor? She didn't hesitate, just dropped the bag over the wall and climbed over herself, sliding down the pole and landing in a flower bed.

Now what? She was in an enclosed back yard with high fences, fences too high to climb over. But there was a table and chairs. She dragged a chair over, stepped onto it, climbed over the wall, and found herself in another enclosed yard, this one possibly belonging to a business of some sort. There was a gate with a bolt, easy to open —and then she was in a passage to the sidewalk. Just like that. But the bodyguard was on that sidewalk.

She stuffed the nightshirt into the bag and slipped back

into her clothes — jeans, T-shirt, a hoodie, and sandals, that was all except for underwear. It was early January, but warm for the last few days. Tonight there was a chill in the air. Even in the hoodie, she was shivering. Feeling for the phone, she cut herself. What else was in that bag? She had a feeling she didn't want to know. She pulled out the money first and counted — $400, way beyond her wildest dreams. That could last awhile. Finally, she found the phone.

Cody imagined herself among the rarest teen-agers in America — those who'd never owned a cell phone. Miguel's girls couldn't have them, absolutely not, that was forbidden, but now and then the older girls, the ones who worked on their own, and the customers — especially the customers — would let them play with their phones as if they were toys.

Cody knew all about Uber, mostly from George, the customer who'd so proudly shown her how he could see where all the drivers were and how long they'd take to get to him, and then they'd both watched, fascinated, as the car he called had turned around and the driver steered it along the route marked in the app. About the best thing she'd ever seen! She sure hoped the freak had Uber. If not, maybe she could download it. With what credit card? she thought.

But the app was there. Matthew would arrive in two minutes. Whew. She used the time to catch her breath and then along came the Mazda the app had predicted. She hurled herself into the car, hoping against hope her guard was looking the other way.

"Wait, you're not Roger," Matthew said.

"Hi, Matthew," she said in her friendliest voice. "I'm his daughter. He left his phone at home and I'm supposed to take it to him."

She had killed a man named Roger.

5

S kip stopped for a salad to go at La Boulangerie — a daintier lunch than usual, but it was January; you had to starve in January — and arrived at the office to find surveillance tapes had already been delivered. The yoga studio didn't have a camera, but the umbrella place did. The victim had walked by at about 10 p.m. January 2, two days ago — and sure enough, he was with a young female wearing jeans and a hoodie. She was in profile, so you couldn't see much of her face, but she had the right hair, it looked like. Actually, you couldn't tell if it was pink on the ends, but there was a lot of it and it looked curly.

He'd walked back without her and then walked by a few more times, almost as if pacing. Other people walked by as well, but Skip had no way to know whether any of them were significant or not.

It sure blew a hole in their theory. Where was the woman all this time? She didn't appear on the tape again.

The last time the victim did was about 11:15, and he looked grim. As if, perhaps, he was about to spray racial slurs on a wall and... what? Try to kill the woman? Who'd killed him instead? It sure looked that way. But why keep her waiting?

If nothing else, Skip thought, this probably placed the time of death. It had to be sometime after 11:15 and her bet was not much after. So the killer would have fled about that time. Or maybe nearer midnight. Good to know.

SHE WAS IMPATIENT, eager to hear from Dustin, but it wasn't like she was going to run out of things to do. She tried googling Namaste Bitch. Aha. Dustin didn't have a website, but she found his inspiration — a pretty funny web series with a way-too-similar name. For the hell of it, Skip watched a few episodes, but, since it didn't star any pink-haired yoginis, went on to the less pleasant chore she had — figuring out all those slurs:

"Blackass bitch spicaninny snigger mexcrement batman diaperhead BMO."

Using her imagination, she saw a little crossover on the first three, and "mexcrement" wasn't that hard. But this was clearly a job for some site like insults.com, and sure enough, she found it: "The Racial Slur Database."

You had to love the Interwebs!

As she suspected, a diaperhead was a raghead — even she knew what that was — and batman wasn't a nun, but a Muslim woman in "cape and mask." A BMO was the same thing, for black moving object, referring to clothes, not skin color.

So — here was all the sexism you could possibly dredge up, along with hate slurs against Africans and African-Americans, Latinas, and Muslims. Where was this guy coming from?

She thought about that a moment, but the answer came quickly and a bit ironically: north Louisiana. Anywhere outside Orleans Parish, really. It had become increasingly clear in recent months that hating those three groups went together; was even, in some circles, somewhat fashionable. The guy might not even have been dangerous. Maybe just another yahoo protesting political correctness, an almost socially acceptable pastime these days.

Wait. Re-cal-cu-lating! He had to be dangerous. Even some idiot who thought hate-speak was okay just because his buddies did it wasn't exactly operating in a violence-free zone.

And now so many of those idiots — yes, definitely idiots; if political correctness was over, like these kinds of guys apparently thought, it was over for her too. She was damn well not mincing her delicate opinions, at least privately. These idiots thought it was okay to throw insults around like peanut hulls. And that had to be dangerous.

Dammit, she was sick of waiting for Dustin to call! She dialed The Lotus Ranch and went medieval on their mindful ass, which worked just fine now that she'd laid the groundwork. The sweet namaste babe at the other end of the line assured her Dustin would call back in ten minutes max.

She checked her email to pass the time and found a note from the coroner: Eureka! Got an ID! She was punching in his number when the phone rang.

Well. Finally!

"Dustin, you're missing all the excitement."

"Hey! You don't sound like a cop."

"Well, I am — I'm a cop telling you to get your namaste ass home ASAP. Although technically I'm not allowed to do that."

"You telling me I messed up?"

"No, I think you've got plenty of other people to do that for you. Your landlord, for one — he seems pretty pissed; maybe the city, unless your illegal short-term rental unit is actually properly registered, but I sincerely doubt that, since your lease says..."

"Oh, shit! You're right. I fucked everything up."

"Dustin! Did anyone mention a man was killed in your apartment?"

"Yeah, they did. Oh, shit! I guess I just thought..."

"You didn't think it was important enough to get your ass on the next plane out of there?"

"Shit. I really fucked up."

"Well, here's a clue. What do you think's the best thing to do now?"

He sighed. "Get my namaste ass home. But could I just register a complaint?"

"Yeah? What?" She wasn't going to let him off the hook.

"You sound like my mama."

"Okay. Complaint registered. One last thing, okay? What agency did you use for that short-term rental January 2?"

"Airbnb. Why?"

Why? WHY? What was wrong with this guy? "Because the guy you rented it to got killed. Do you not get that?"

"Ohhhh, shit!"

"What's his name, Dustin?"

"I'm supposed to remember that?"

"Come on, you must have a contract or something. At least an email."

"Look I don't have my laptop with me. I don't even have a cell phone! I came here to enrich my spiritual life and I left all that behind. Do you even understand that?"

I understand you're a spoiled-beyond-belief brat.

"Could you just get home and figure it out so we can, you know, solve the murder that took place in the place where you sleep!"

"I don't sleep there, I..."

"Yeah, you're running an illegal hotel. Plus an illegal business, probably. Do you even have a license for that studio of yours?"

"You know what, Sergeant? I don't like your attitude. I think I'll report you to Internal Affairs."

"We call it the Public Integrity Bureau. Namaste." It had been deliciously tempting to say "Namaste, bitch", but that wouldn't go down well with Public Integrity.

CODY HADN'T ACTUALLY ENTERED a destination — she'd been in such a rush she'd just selected something from the menu of Roger's past destinations. "Hey, can you just drop me in the French Quarter?" she said.

"You changing your destination? You know that might cost your dad extra, right?

"That's ok. I made a mistake."

"Where in the French Quarter?"

"Oh, wait! You know what's good?" She named a hotel where she'd tricked, a really busy one on the edge of the Quarter. "My dad works at the restaurant down the street."

"The Palace? I could drop you there."

"Okay, sure, that's great. Do I have to do anything?"

"I'll do it." He adjusted his app.

"So. You live on Magazine Street?"

"No, just off it. I was going to walk uptown, but then I got tired."

"Downtown."

"What?"

"Uptown's where I picked you up. We're going downtown now. You must have just moved here."

"Yeah, we did. Actually, this week."

"So. What school you going to?"

School. What a concept. Kids her age went to school. She'd almost forgotten.

"St. Joseph's," she said, naming her old school, back in the parish. There was always a St. Joseph's. But she realized she'd better get hold of this conversation fast. For her, the simplest questions were unanswerable, required time to think up lies, might even require information about — well, just about anything — that she didn't have. The girls weren't allowed online. They were allowed to watch a certain amount of television, and they had DVD's, mostly Disney ones, but they could never actually go out to movies, and the only people they had to talk to were their customers, who weren't usually very interested in conversation.

If Cody really thought about it, she wasn't even sure who the president was. There'd been an election, she knew that, so maybe it was someone new, not Obama any more. *I used to be a good student!* She had made all B's last time. Thinking about it made her tear up.

"How long have you been driving for Uber?" she asked. From now on, it ought to be easy. The trick was to get the *putero* to talk about himself.

When he let her out in front of The Palace, Cody felt disoriented. Even though she'd been living in Houston — a big city, everyone said — it never seemed to have any particular center. Not like this. This was all lights and crowds. But she did remember it. It was at least a little familiar.

More disorienting still was the sensation of being on her own, not being watched all the time, having no place to go that wasn't her own decision, actually being...free. She was trying hard to grasp it, just to breathe the air that was once more hers alone, however briefly. She knew she'd traded a life of slavery for life in prison but for now, maybe just for a few days — she was nobody's human but her own.

And she had a plan. She really did have a friend named Terry, although she looked nothing like Kristen Stewart.

Terry had escaped. She'd gotten a trick to help her—probably blackmailed him, Cody thought. He'd gotten her a ride to New Orleans, where he knew someone who had a job for her. All this she told Cody in advance — but had it really happened?

Cody had to believe. She just had to!

She went into the restaurant, The Palace Café, in case Matthew remembered her, and also to go to the bathroom. The girl in the mirror looked... well, she looked like she'd been through it. She needed new clothes, at least a comb... what was in that gym bag?

She took it into a stall to look. And what she saw there was so frightening, so downright horrifying considering what she'd just been through, that she just left it right there in the bathroom, night shirt and all. All she took was the money, which she put in her shoe except for ten dollars in a pocket.

On the way out, she exchanged her hoodie for a warm-looking fleece jacket someone had hung on a hook, and it proved to have a comb in the pocket. Her lucky day — that saved a trip to the drugstore.

"Which way to Bourbon Street?" she asked the first person she saw, and she was on her way.

She'd been there before, at least seen it from a distance when she was a kid, before her mother had completely folded on her. She and her mom and Maw-Maw all came to

New Orleans once, just to have lunch and look around. And then eat beignets, the best part! She'd loved the way people played music in the park by the church. And in the outdoor restaurants near the river. It was one of the best memories of her childhood.

But nothing prepared her for Bourbon Street at night — and not just any night, but the night of a bowl game. She felt almost physically assaulted by the throngs. And the music that came from some of the clubs — the deafening, pounding, thundering music that wasn't anything like the music by the river. But mostly what spooked her was the feeling of chaos, of everything just hanging by a thread.

She supposed that had a lot to do with the drinks in everyone's hand and the fact that most people were either talking too loud or outright screaming. It made her want to run, but she knew this was the safest place she could be.

One thing she knew — not to talk to any men. That was going to be nothing but trouble. She tried accosting a girl about her own age. "Hey, can you tell me where the strip clubs are?" The girl laughed in her face. But how was that funny?

She walked. Maybe that was the best thing, just to walk until she thought of something better to do. Eventually, she came to a section where the quality of the street life was different. It wasn't so crowded and it was mostly men. It dawned on her that this must be a gay area. That could only be good, for her purposes. By now it was nearly midnight and she was starving. And for once, she had plenty of money. She went in a place called the Clover Grill, thinking to get a burger, and pretty much fell in love instantly.

She sat at the counter, watching the cooks. It was just about the best place she'd ever been. People here were loud too, but they were funny. And friendly. The best part was no one hit on her. Either everyone was on a date, it seemed, or gay. And also on a date. It was easy to start conversations with people, and not a single person laughed when she asked where the strip joints were.

"Fuhgeddaboutit!" said Elliott, her new best friend. "Baby, you are way too young to be dancing in one of those places!" Elliott wore jeans and a white wifebeater, and had more tattoos than Johnny Depp. He didn't look a lot older than she was.

"You're a runaway, right?" asked his friend, red-headed Mikey. "We could take you to Covenant House. It's a place you can go where they won't... you know... turn you in."

"He means they won't call the police," Elliot clarified. "You could stay there, at least tonight."

Cody filed that as a possible last resort. "Good to know," she said, "but I've got a friend. All I have to do is find her."

"Well, honey, no problem —" Elliott made a panoramic gesture — "there's hardly anybody in town tonight."

"She's a dancer."

"Oh. Hence the strip club question."

"Elementary, Holmes," said Mikey, but Cody had no idea what that was code for.

Elliott sighed. "Did she tell you what club?"

Cody scrunched up her face, trying to remember. "She did, but... I don't know, something with... 'girls' in it, maybe?"

The guys laughed. "Well, that eliminates Rick's Cabaret, anyway. Was it R-Rated Girls?"

"I don't think so..."

"Is this kid young, like you?"

"Maybe a little older."

"Daddy's Girls then," Mikey said. "They hire all the young ones."

"Yes!" Cody squealed. "That's it!"

Elliot said, "Ewwwwww."

"What?" asked Mikey, "the name or the concept?"

"That was for the name. I'm not even gonna comment on the concept." He gave Cody the side-eye. She was pretty sure she knew why, but she wished she knew what "concept" was. Well, never mind about that now, she had to think of a way to get into Daddy's Girls.

"How are you planning to get in?" Mikey said, as if he'd overheard her thinking. "Got a fake ID?"

"No, I thought... you think the guy at the door would find Terry for me?"

Elliott and Mikey looked at one another, till Elliott raised an eyebrow. "Maybe," he said.

"But if he does, who's going to take care of the door?"

And suddenly Cody remembered she wasn't powerless — because she had $400 in her shoe. "Hey, could I hire you two guys to find her?"

Elliott stared. "Huh?"

"What about if we all walk down there and you guys go in and get her. I'll give you fifty bucks."

They stared at each other again. "What about the cover charge?"

Before she could stop herself, she asked, "What's that?"

"Oh, brudda," Elliott said. "Looks like she needs a mama."

Cody slipped off her stool and stood tall. "If you're just going to make fun of me..."

"We're not making fun of you, we're trying to take care of you. Forget the fifty bucks. You need freakin' help. Sure we'll take you down there." He looked at Mikey for confirmation.

Mikey nodded. "We're definitely not leaving her here. I mean, if she were a Pomeranian we wouldn't, right?"

She didn't know what that was, either, but the "leaving" part was okay with her. She hadn't seen Terry in months. She wished she looked better. "Hey, does this place have a bathroom?"

"It must, but..."

"Yeah, it's a pretty small joint. That's ok. Whatever it's like, I can handle it." She called to the cooks, "You guys got a bathroom?"

One of them stared at her, looking dubious. Finally pointed with his thumb.

Cody followed the thumb, washed her face, and ran her found comb through her hair.

"Ok, ready," she said to her new temporary parents. "How about if I pay for your burgers?"

Elliott said, "You're a nice kid, you know that? But no." She felt her eyes go glossy. "Hey what's wrong?"

"Nothing. I just... I guess I'm just tired." But it wasn't nothing. It was the casual compliment, like she was a person instead of a... thing. A means to an end. A piece of furniture that could fuck.

6

The dead man was Benjamin Solo, last known address in Houston, Texas, multiple arrests for pimping and pandering. But he must have been living in New Orleans lately. His wife had reported him missing. Who knew pimps had wives?

This, Skip thought, made for a different theory indeed. It now looked to her like a prostitute had killed her pimp, possibly in self-defense considering what he'd written on the wall.

And yet... if he'd meant to kill her, how did he plan to do it, since no weapons were found? Strangling, maybe. Suffocation.

Skip couldn't shake the feeling that something had been removed from the scene. How had he brought those handcuffs? In his pockets, maybe.

Abasolo was sitting at his desk, looking bored although he probably had a ton of work to do. "Hey, AA," she said, "I got an ID on the freak. He's a pimp, formerly from Houston. Late of New Orleans."

"That makes sense. These guys run in girls for all the bowl games — well, probably for all the Saints games too."

"Yeah. That short-term rental thing makes a lot of sense — probably cheaper than a hotel, not nearly as much stuff can go wrong, and the johns stand less chance of running into their brother-in-law."

He was staring off into space, evidently putting something together. "I like the anonymity angle." He turned to her. "It's all done online. You just use a fake credit card — how hard is it to get that? — maybe arrange with the owner to leave the key somewhere, and you're untraceable. Nobody sees you, nobody sees your girls, nobody sees the johns. Beautiful set-up! What name did he use, by the way?"

"Due to religious fervor, I don't have that yet."

"Come again?"

"The tenant's on his way back from a religious retreat. I did find out the service was Airbnb, but assuming Benjy rented it, it probably doesn't matter what name he used."

"Benjy?"

She shrugged.

"Maybe the john rented it."

The john. He was right. There had to be a john. Which meant that person was missing, and more important, the woman was missing. Skip's stomach flipped over. "I've got to call Read. You want to go out with me today? See what we can dig up on Benjy?

"I thought you'd never ask."

She got Read on the horn. "Hey, Perm, we never talked about a third person in that yoga joint."

"Don't call me that!"

"You're right. Permy's better." Read squealed. She was on a campaign to get people to call her "Melia", which she pronounced Ma-LEE-a, but "Permy" was way too much fun.

"Listen, we've got the dead man — Benjamin Solo, did you hear? — and we've got the pink-haired beauty, but... any more hairs or fibers? I feel like there was somebody else."

"Well, we know there was Dustin..."

"I meant besides Dustin."

"Okay then." Suddenly her voice had a lot of confidence. "We found a lot of dark hairs that matched some others in a brush in the bedroom, and also just in various vacuumings around the house. Presumed to be Dustin's. Prints also, although we can't be sure till Dustin gets back from Lotusland. I mean, he did live there, right, before he turned that place into an Airbnbad?"

"I'm gonna take that as a value judgment."

"You got that right! They're all over my neighborhood — don't get me started."

"To answer your question — yes, we think he did live there, at least for a while. You find anything else?"

"Nothing significant. Various other hairs and fibers, like if you had a bunch of yoga students coming in and out, you know? But nothing in the bed, and nothing particularly indicating another person was near the victim. Well, except for the blood. We already talked about that."

"Right. Not Benjy's blood. We thought it was the woman's — if she's the killer."

"Yeah? What's wrong with that?"

"Well, maybe she's not."

Skip was glad to have Abasolo with her when she broke the news to Mrs. Solo. It was always the job of the lead homicide investigator to notify next of kin and, predictably, it was the least desirable part of the job if you didn't count the smells.

Mrs. Solo lived in a run-down apartment complex near Fat City that was a virtual Latino neighborhood, but she wasn't precisely Mrs. Solo, it seemed, although there was one, they learned, but she lived in another city; or perhaps another country. Gloria Bustillo wasn't sure. And Gloria might as well have been Mrs. Solo — she was the mother of the two-year-old hanging onto her legs, and Benjamin's co-parent as well as co-tenant.

The apartment was sparsely furnished, probably with cast-offs, but it was neat and, with the help of some Mexican tablecloths Gloria used for throws, quite cheerful.

Gloria herself was a nice Mestiza lady — round and a bit plain; very serious. Not an entirely happy person, Skip suspected.

They broke the news of her partner's death and asked her to come to the morgue for a formal I.D., where she was stoic, mostly, but cried a little. After that, delicate questions arose.

"Would it be ok if I called you Gloria?" Skip asked and, granted permission, asked, "Gloria, do you have a job?"

"Oh, no! I'm a full-time mom."

"Before that?" She watched for hesitation or cast-down eyes, wondering if Gloria'd been one of Benjamin's hookers, but Gloria answered immediately. "I worked in the laundry my parents own. That's where I met Benny." She said his name in an adorably affectionate way, a bit drawn out, like "Bennn-nie". Skip really hated this part of the job. Watching it sink in that someone was gone.

"Can you tell us what Benny did for a living?"

"Of course. He works in construction. And sometimes with friends; he helped friends with little jobs."

"What kind of little jobs?"

She shrugged. "Helping people move; hauling. Painting sometimes. Handyman kinds of things."

Could she really not know she was living with a pimp? Abasolo said, "Do you know if he was involved with any criminal activity?"

Her eyes darted. And dilated. Sure she knew. "I know he used to be," she said carefully.

Skip showed her a photo taken from the surveillance camera next door. "Is this your boy friend?"

"Yes. Who is that woman?"

"That's what we're trying to find out. Look closely. Do you recognize her?"

She shook her head.

Skip said, "We believe he was killed on January 2. Did he tell you where he was going that night?"

Her face tightened with grief. "The day of the Sugar Bowl. The last day I saw him. He said he had a job to do. With an old friend from Houston, Miguel Bustamente. They were moving furniture for someone, I think. Miguel said they went out afterwards, and he said Benny— they got separated..." she teared up. "I never saw him again."

"You're in touch with Miguel?"

She looked uncomfortable, squirmy even. "He calls every day. His sister is missing too. He's frantic, trying to find her."

"Is that his sister in the picture?"

"Perhaps," she said, her body language saying, No! It's the puta who killed my man! She probably knew the girl was a literal puta.

"Do you have Miguel's address in Houston?"

She looked surprised. "He's not there, he's still here. Looking for his sister and Benjamin. I don't know where he stays, though." She thought a moment. "But Carlos might. Try Carlos."

And she gave them the address of yet a third pimp — or so Skip assumed.

But it turned out Carlos was Gloria's brother, who had a perfectly legit job in construction and a pretty good idea where to find Miguel — at a dive bar in Mid City, probably later that night.

"Hey, look at this," Skip said as they were driving back to the Second. "Read just texted me. She's got something good for us."

"Permy, you da man!" Skip texted back.

Read was waiting for them, a blue gym bag and a plastic shopping bag on Skip's desk, a box of latex gloves at the ready. "Look what I've got." Pulling on a pair of the gloves, she removed from the bag an array of terrifying-looking knives, of the sort you might use for butchering, Skip thought. And then there were some delicate, dainty ones that gave her further pause.

Abasolo whistled.

Skip said, "What are we looking at?" Slipping on gloves, she touched a blade. "Yow. Nasty."

Read was grinning canary feathers. "I think these are the knives someone used on that poor dog."

Abasolo said, "What?"

"Sheba," Read said impatiently. "The original 'blackass bitch'."

"Oh. How did I forget that?"

"The knives had been sterilized, but we found blood inside the gym bag — and it was the bitch's blood. No disrespect intended."

Skip saw Abasolo trying not to smile. "I'm sure none would be taken. By the nice lady dog."

Read gave him a quizzical look. "Are you flirting?"

"Are you kidding? We're all doing a job here."

Skip was pretty sure she saw just the tiniest bit of pink bleeding into his complexion. Everyone flirted with Read, even when they didn't mean to.

But Read was irritated. "Hey, this is big, dudes! You realize what he was going to do to that girl?"

"Hey, babe, not so fast," Skip said. "What does this have to do with our girl?"

Read held up a baggie with several hairs in it. "Found these in the bag too. See that?" She pointed with a pencil at the pink ends. "Same hairs we found at the yoga joint."

"Just... under the knives? Or what?"

"Well, there's another surprise." She opened the shopping bag. "They were on this." The item was a garment in a clear zipped plastic bag, which she removed and held up.

Whatever Skip had been expecting, it wasn't this. It was a nightshirt or possibly a long T-shirt, in a playful design, meant for a smallish woman, maybe even a kid.

"That was in the bag?" Skip said.

"Stuffed on top of the knives. All wadded up."

"Whatehell is it?" Abasolo said. The nightshirt was a bright turquoise color with a tuckered-looking cartoon cat on it, the legend "CAT NAP!" printed at the top. The cat's face and neck were stained with blood. "Is it for a kid?"

Read made a face. "Could be. But it's a woman's size."

"Women do wear them," Skip said, trying to remain sphinx-like regarding her own nocturnal apparel. As it happened, she owned several similar garments. "But not usually hookers, I imagine."

"Unless the john wanted them to. And judging from the blood, it looks like this john did."

There they were. Back to "the john."

"Do we really think Benny did this?" she said. "I mean, the john could have been the other guy's customer — Miguel — but we know Benny's got a record for pimping. Why would he need another pimp? It sure looks like there was a third person there."

"Yeah," Read said. "But I can't find any evidence..."

"Well..." Skip held up her own gloved hands. "Gloves? Condoms? There might not be any." Her phone vibrated. Looking at it, she said, "Excuse me a minute. It's the coroner's office."

When she returned, Abasolo was asking, "Where'd this stuff come from anyway?"

"Well, now, that part's interesting," Read said. "Someone found it yesterday — in the ladies' room at the Palace Café. It might have been left January 2, which we're still postulating is the day of the murder, right?"

"Yes," Abasolo said. "But whoa! Whole new scenario. Hooker fights with Benny, kills him, steals his weapons, and flees to The Palace Café, where she leaves the weapons? What's up with all that?"

Skip rejoined them. "The Palace Café?"

They caught her up, and she said, "I've got some news too. If she did kill Benny, I sure don't see how. The word I just got is the coroner thinks he died from asphyxiation."

They were silent for a moment. Finally, Read said, "Come again? You mean like a plastic bag over the head?"

"Sure. Or a chokehold. But he didn't have a broken hyoid bone. He did have some bruising."

"Is that something a smallish woman could have done?"

Skip shrugged. "I guess. If he was already unconscious. But there is that bruising. If it were me, I'd go for a pillow over the face instead of the chokehold. But why do it at all? If she's fighting for her life and she manages to knock him out, why kill him? Why not just walk out the door, go into the nearest restaurant, and dial 911? I mean, the guy was trying to kill her. Isn't that what we think?"

"You know why she didn't," Abasolo said.

Of course she did. "You mean because she's young, female, and scared? And no one likes cops? Oh, right, I forgot. I should have just become a brain surgeon."

Read said. "Or maybe a rock star."

"She is a rock star," Abasolo said, almost causing Skip to tear up. She'd been in this department a long time and her male colleagues hadn't always made it easy for her.

She couldn't get the hooker out of her head. There had to be a customer. And if there was, either he or the hooker had killed Benny. But no matter who the killer was, both hooker and john were missing. What if they were together? Skip's scalp prickled.

If the john had somehow managed to kill Benny and kidnap the hooker, she was probably already dead. Or soon would be.

She thought this guy hadn't yet worked up to killing, but he was headed that way. Surely he hadn't intended to leave the girl alive after he tortured her. Or were the whips and restraints meant only for fun and games? She couldn't bring herself to buy that. The injured dog haunted her.

"Langdon... you okay?"

She focused, suddenly realizing how tired she was.

A.A. looked at his watch. "Enough of this crap. I'm going home. Anybody want to get a drink?"

It was way past time for Skip's shift to end and she didn't see any point hanging around. "No, thanks," she said. "Steve's making dinner. With any luck."

But Read turned to Abasolo. "You buyin'?" she asked hopefully.

STEVE WAS INDEED MAKING DINNER, having a lot of fun, it looked like, with some sort of beef stew thing. "Hi, chef!"

They were about to kiss, but Rambla intervened. She never saw any reason why someone else should get affection before she did. They both laughed. Skip looked at her warm, rustic, more or less accidentally minimalist kitchen with its bear-like chef and felt there was no place she'd rather be. She almost hated being this comfortable — something was bound to get in her way, and sure enough, Steve's move-to-L.A. talk was bumming her out.

"How was work?" His love was documentary filmmaking, but he did film editing to supplement whatever that brought in. And that was the current problem — as the Louisiana film industry had dried up, so had his work.

"Fine," he said. "But we're nearly finished."

"Anything else on the horizon?" She was hoping against hope.

"Well... no. I hate to say it, babe, but I think I've just got to go to L.A. and scare something up."

"But that would mean..."

"Yeah. It would really screw up our life."

She shook her head, as if to banish the whole idea. "I can't even stand to talk about it. I just had a really... let's say...full day at work. I could sure use a walk," she said, "and I'm sure you-know-who could." She picked up Rambla's leash. "You want to join us?"

"Sure."

She'd been pretty sure he would. It was one of her favorite things they did together. "Let me just get out of my sergeant drag." Quickly, she exchanged her dark pants and blazer for loose-fitting jeans and a sweater.

"Can I start with Rambla?"

"Okay."

They took turns being the walker. When they were underway, he said, "Actually I know about your, let's say... full work day. I heard you got a pretty interesting case."

"Oh, come on! No way you could know that."

"Are you kidding? Dead guy in a yoga studio? That's not your usual gangbanger drive-by. It was all over nola.com."

"How'd you know it was my case?"

"Oh... well... that was too."

"Damn! I'm gonna kill Sergeant McAvoy." The sometimes over-zealous press officer. "Well. It actually is an interesting case, and it would especially interest you."

"How's that?"

"It involves your favorite subject."

"Canine Communication?" The subject of the documentary for which he was currently trying to find investors.

"Try again."

"Got it! Cooking for two."

"No, but thrilled to hear that's on the list. Think darker."

"Film noir?"

"Maybe I should have said your least favorite thing. What's the scourge of the cities and the beginning of the end of neighborhoods as we know them?" She was pretty much quoting him.

If he'd been Rambla she'd have actually seen his ears prick up. She still wasn't sure she didn't. "You're telling me somebody murdered short-term rentals?"

"Ha! You wish."

"Come on, you know you do too."

"Okay, I do too. But no, no white knight came charging in and singlehandedly wiped them out. On the other hand, there could be a cautionary tale for renters here. What's a perfect place to commit a murder?"

"I don't know. Someplace nobody knows you or the victim; preferably off the streets. Wait a minute! When you rent from Airbnb, they never see you, right?"

"Now you're getting somewhere."

"Somebody got killed in a short-term rental unit? Hey, it's a perfect set-up — I mean, if it's premeditated."

"Will you stop sniffing and start walking?" she said to Rambla. "With all the stuff you hate about Airbnb, you never thought of that one, did you? Ideal crime scene. You don't even have to dispose of the body — it becomes someone else's problem."

"Are you telling me someone actually rented an apartment to commit a murder in?"

"Sure looks like it."

"Wow. Pretty ingenious."

Skip sighed. "Maybe pretty inevitable. Remember the Axeman?"

"Oh, definitely. Murder in the Twelve-Step Programs — one of your most celebrated cases."

"Anonymity is a beautiful thing for a criminal. And not so beautiful for us."

"I'm trying to get this to sink in. I think we've got to call the TV stations right now! And nola.com."

"What are you talking about?"

"They've got to stop calling it the Namaste Murder and move onto Short-Term Murder. That's much better."

"Well, of course you'd think so. It's definitely bad press for Airbnbad. Nobody wants their house to become a killing field."

And if the truth were told, she didn't hate the idea either. Back when short-term rentals were illegal, they were eating

New Orleans alive. Jimmy Dee and Lane were practically the only people left who actually lived on their block — everyone else had moved out to take advantage of the new, quick-profit opportunity that had suddenly appeared before their eyes. The thing Dustin had done was actually pretty typical, in one sense — people had moved back home with their parents or other relatives so they could rent out their own places. He'd just put a twist on it by renting out a place he rented.

Worse, downright sinister so far as Steve was concerned, were the people — often out-of-towners — who bought up entire apartment buildings and evicted the tenants to run what was actually an illegal hotel. Or even bought as many single-family homes as they could gobble up. Not a problem many places — but for a heavy-duty tourist city like New Orleans where rentals were at a premium anyway, it could quickly erode the most historic and desirable neighborhoods. Fragile areas like the Quarter and the Marigny were in danger of losing their neighborhood identity to become de facto hotel districts.

But the city had recently legalized the phenomenon in order to be able to regulate it. It was too early to see how that was going to work, but the good news was that short-terms had been almost completely banned in the French Quarter.

Jimmy Dee was ecstatic — although with reservations. "I'm going to throw a block party to celebrate," he said, "if anyone actually moves back to the block."

ody and her two new best friends stood awkwardly at the door of Daddy's Girls. She hadn't told Elliott and Mikey she had no I.D. at all, not even a fake one, and she didn't want them to know. Finally, she blurted to the bouncer, "Do you know Terry Locke?"

"Yeah, she dances here."

"Can I see her?"

"Well, that would be pretty hard if I can't let you in, right?"

"I'll go," Elliott said. "Mikey, you wait with Coe."

Coe. Now she had a nickname. She liked that.

The door guy looked disappointed and she wondered if he expected her to bribe him. She didn't have a clue how those things worked. But she paid the cover charge — having quickly learned what that was — and Elliott slipped into the smoky sea of humanity, muttering, "Good-bye, cruel world."

While they waited, Mikey grilled her. She didn't know whether he was making small talk or had some more sinister reason, but she sure didn't want to hurt his feelings, so what to do? She didn't think she should tell him anything, but the truth was, she'd led such a sheltered life in a very weird way she didn't have enough material to lie properly. One of the girls was from Atlanta, though. That ought to work. So she said that was where she was from and she pulled out St. Joseph's School again. Yeah, she was a runaway, she admitted, and that was a lie too.

He'd been one too, he said, when his parents found out he was gay. But now everything was fine. They all got along, and he'd moved back in with them. He and Elliott were best friends, not partners or anything, though, and why was it so hard to fall in love with your best friend?

She ventured, "Cause you know too much about each other?" and he laughed.

"You're a pretty smart kid! How old are you, anyhow?"

"Seventeen," she was about to say, which was not remotely true, but then Elliott came back. "She'll meet us here in an hour," he said. "She's got a break then."

"Well, let's go to the river. We sure can't take babycakes here to a bar."

"You guys don't have to stay with me. I'm good."

"Oh, yes. Yes, we definitely do. You are so not going to wander around the French Quarter at midnight alone."

She had a paranoid flash. This wasn't possible! They were way too nice. Were they going to roll her at the river? Had they figured out she had money?

But she went. She was too tired to argue and anyhow, what if they did? It was almost worth it to feel like this for a little bit — as if she had real friends — even if the whole thing was fake.

At the end of the hour, though, she still had all her money and she knew a great deal more about them than they did about her — she hoped. But she was pretty sure she'd kept them on the subject of themselves and what it was like to be gay in a small town or suburb, and then come out and find a community in New Orleans. She'd also learned Elliott was a server in a really fancy restaurant and Mikey was a bartender in a dive bar. She took careful note of the names, wondering if she'd need to find these guys again.

Terry came out squealing, wearing jeans and a sloppy old sweatshirt, under which Cody could see a sequinned strap. "Coco!" She grabbed Cody in what would have been a bear hug if she were big enough. She was a petite redhead, even smaller than Cody, the last person you'd expect to find stripping. "Baby, baby, baby! I didn't think you were gonna make it."

Oh, Lord, as her Maw-Maw would say. What were Elliott and Mikey going to make of that? "Let me just say good-bye to my friends, okay?"

Elliott looked as worried as if he were her mama, sending her off to first grade. "Miss Thing, you call if you need anything, ya hear? Take my phone number."

"I — uh — well, I don't have a phone."

"Well, Terry will. Here, I've got a card — it's got my number on it."

Mikey handed him a pen. "Put mine on it too."

She took the card and then, after many thank-yous and exchanges of good wishes, Cody was back in her own world, the one she and Terry had shared. "He brought us here for the Sugar Bowl," she said, "you know that fleabag place we stayed that other time? Instant replay. Except I... well, a customer passed out on me and I got away."

"Just now?"

"About three hours ago."

"Oh, God. Miguel doesn't know where I am, right?"

"Are you crazy? I'd never tell him something like that." Terry had escaped and that made her a hero to the other girls.

"Anybody know where you are?"

"No, of course not. Only my babysitters — the guys you just met. That's what they called themselves. I met them in a burger joint. No way they could run into Miguel."

"Okay, good. You need a place to stay?"

Cody's knees buckled with relief. "Ohhhh, thank you! I can pay too."

"How'd you get money?"

"Rolled the trick." She made herself grin, as if the trick wasn't dead at the time.

Terry nodded approvingly. "Good move. I'm going to take you inside. There's a place in the back where you can wait for me. Sometimes somebody has a sick kid, so we keep a place to lie down. We also have beds in the private rooms, but I don't want to take the risk of someone walking in on you. How would that be?"

Cody was pretty sure she managed to nod, but not positive. Maybe she just thought she had. Now that it was all over, she was so tired she could barely walk. Her eyes closed the minute her head hit the stained sofa.

She woke up briefly while Terry wrestled her into a car and then her apartment and then onto another sofa, still with her clothes on. And the next time she woke up, someone was fondling the newly-rescued area Miguel had been peddling for the last two years. This kind of thing had happened before, but she remembered yesterday perfectly well. She'd gotten away. Nobody could do that now — she'd killed a man to get her body back.

Furious — not even scared, just plain mad — she flipped her eyes open and found herself staring at a strange man. She couldn't help it, she screamed. The man straightened up fast and pulled the cover back over her. "Bad dream?" he asked, as if nothing had happened, glancing at some place Cody couldn't see — no doubt Terry's bedroom.

She sat up so she'd feel less vulnerable, and, as Terry walked into the room, already fully dressed, the man slinked into the kitchen, where he began opening cabinets and pulling out cereal boxes. He contemplated Cody from there. "So! You're Cordelia, right? Welcome to our home."

"Hi, toots," Terry said, "how'd you sleep? This is Winston. My boy friend."

Oh, joy. A rapeophile boy friend.

Winston said, "How about some breakfast?"

"How about some coffee?" Terry said, and that was what she wanted to hear.

"I'm in. Hi, Winston." She gave him her most evil look, which required a bit of staring. He was handsome enough, she thought — about five eight, not all that much bigger than Terry, African-American, awesome dreads, nice sweater and jeans, not that baggy ass-crack look. He didn't look like the low-life she'd already decided he was, he looked like he could be a musician, but he was probably some kind of service industry drudge. Or maybe a gangster who dressed better than most.

"Good to meet you, babe. Gotta bone out. Catch you later?"

He brushed Terry's lips with his and practically flew out the door. Embarrassed, she hoped. Terry looked at her watch. "Late for class. He's at Delgado — in computer... ummm, something." You could see the pride all over her pert, pretty little face.

Terry thought she had a good man, and maybe she did.

Maybe he wasn't really like that, maybe he... naaah, he was like that. Which meant she couldn't stay there.

Terry handed her a cup of coffee and sat down in the neat, small living room with her. "I'm so happy you got out! Tell me everything."

Cody shrugged. "Okay. I planned it. When I found out we were coming here, I knew I could do it if you'd put me up for one night..."

"Baby, you can stay as long as you like. You know that." Terry really was a nice chick. At one time she'd been almost a mother to Cody, helping her deal with the pain and the depression and the loss — the many losses. Oh, the losses. Family. Freedom. Her whole life, really; any sense of worth she might have had. Cody'd at first numbed the pain with drugs from Miguel, and Terry had helped her; then she'd helped her gradually get off the drugs. Things happened with the girls that Miguel couldn't control. They became friends. They were all each other had. And now and then one of them made it out and helped another. Kind of a teen-age hooker underground railroad.

Terry had held her like a mother and said, "You'll make it, CoCo; I know you will. You're little, but you're strong. You're way stronger than you think." She'd said things like that over and over to her until Cody almost believed it. She thought now that she'd be dead if it hadn't been for Terry.

"My family's here, did you know that? In Houma."

"Oh. Well, you're still welcome to stay. So how did you plan your escape?"

"I got hold of a roofie, and fed it to the client."

"But Miguel always..."

"I got lucky. There was a back way out. He never knew I was gone until... well, he still might not know." She just hoped he wouldn't kill Benny the bodyguard once he found out.

Terry fixed some breakfast — although it was actually lunchtime, due to her late-night schedule — and they traded news as they ate, Cody becoming more and more disturbed as Terry's unfolded. Terry was using again. And there was Winston. And the demeaning dancing gig. She wanted to help her, be the rock for Terry that the older girl had been for her, but she had no illusions she really could. She was barely sixteen and wanted for murder. She couldn't help anybody, wasn't sure she'd even make it to her Maw-Maw before she got arrested.

For the first time she realized how sad she was about that.

Soon after they ate, Terry said she had to go to the store to get some food for dinner, although she didn't ask Cody to go with her. Cody thought maybe she was going out to score. "Let me buy the groceries," she said, and pulled out four twenties.

"Oh, baby, no!" Terry howled. But she took two of them. And before she left, she gave Cody a towel and a pair of clean underpants, another small, kind gesture that almost made her cry, it reminded her so vividly of what she'd been missing.

When Terry had gone, Cody took a long hot shower — she'd been absolutely dying for that — and then, feeling guilty as hell, tossed the house for anything she could lift. She found $100, a fake ID, and, in one of Winston's drawers a gun, a whole lot of pills, and a baggie of what looked heroin. She wouldn't be surprised if he was dealing — she already knew he wasn't the angel Terry thought he was.

She fingered the ID, left over from Terry's younger days, which weren't that far away. It said she was Lucy Valdez, a

weird name for a redhead, but the girl in the picture wasn't a
redhead — looked nothing like Terry, in fact. If it worked for
her, it could work for me, she thought, and shoved it in her
pocket.

The gun wouldn't fit, so she left that, hoping she
wouldn't regret it. She couldn't see having the nerve to use it
anyhow. That was Maw-Maw's department — she never
went anywhere without one.

The drugs didn't interest her at all.

She picked up the money and caressed it, wanting it
desperately, but thinking how good Terry had been to her.
She couldn't take it. Could she? I have to, she thought. How
else am I going to get money? And anyway, once she got
a job...

An interesting thought. A job. She wondered, almost for
the first time, if there was a way to avoid going to prison.
Maybe; you never knew. If she made it, she could write
Terry a note thanking her and saying she was sorry for the
unauthorized loan. Unauthorized loan! Terry would get a
kick out of that.

A hundred dollars richer, she went out to explore the
'hood, feeling, as her mother used to say, "almost human
again". When applied to herself, it took on a whole different
meaning. She'd been literally living as a sub-human organ-
ism. It was amazing what a difference a day made.

The neighborhood seemed to be almost all black and
somewhat rundown — no big high-rises, just small, mostly
stucco houses of the type she'd heard called "bungalows."
Mostly, they didn't have yards, just jutted onto the sidewalk,
and also didn't have new paint jobs. She could see people
here weren't doing all that well and she needed someone
like that right now. The question was, who could she trust?
Somebody smaller than she was would be good. She went

into a corner store and bought some jerky. "Good protein", her mother used to say. Often it was her entire dinner or lunch.

The man behind the counter — a portly dude about seventy — had a gruff manner, but kind eyes. She decided to trust the eyes. "Is there a high school around here?"

"Why you wanna know?" he snapped.

"I need to get somewhere," she said. "I thought maybe I could hire a student."

"School goin' on right now," he said. "How you gon' hire somebody in class?"

"I could wait till after school?"

"Why ain't you in school yaself, little miss?"

It took her a minute to think of a decent lie. "My mama's sick today and I've gotta run some errands for her."

"Everybody's got a story, don't they?" He made a tent of one of his eyebrows. "Where ya need to go?"

She sure didn't want to tell anybody. "Lockport," she said. Not that there was that much difference in Lockport and Houma. "I need to go pick up my aunt to take care of Mom."

"How much you gon' pay?"

"Fifty dollars be okay?"

He frowned, thinking. "Might be." He turned toward the back of the store and yelled, "Lamar, git yo' lazy ass out here."

Out came a dude in his 20s, so sketchy-looking there was no way she was ever getting in a car with him — sloppy, sullen, and sporting the butt-crack look. "This lady give you fifty dollars to drive her to Lockport."

"I ain't got no car."

The counter man handed over a set of keys. "Take mine. And you better be back in two hours flat or I send the

Highway Patrol after y'all." He turned back to Cody. "Look at me, young lady. This my nephew, Lamar Clark. He don' look like much, but he a decent kid. You know why I'm doing this?"

Cody shook her head. The truth was, she was mystified. "'Cause you gon' get yo' young ass in trouble if you don't watch out." He winked. "And Lamar's gon' split that fifty with me."

Lamar flashed anger, again giving Cody qualms, but she kept quiet. No need to make him madder.

"I'm Solomon Clark. What's yo' name?"

"Lucy," she said. "Lucy Valdez." And in a minute realized she was still in Terry's neighborhood. She could have kicked herself.

"In a pig's eye," Solomon Clark said. "You ain't no Lucy Valdez. Lamar, you be careful, ya hear?"

Lamar radiated fury — at what, Cody didn't know. She knew she could probably get him out of his mood, but she made an executive decision about her few days of freedom — being nice, since it was no longer required to keep from getting beaten, was no longer on her agenda. Let him be mad! She could tough it out for the next hour or so.

He stunk of cigarette smoke and so did Solomon's car, but she couldn't get the window open.

"Would you mind if we had some air?"

"Whassa matter — you think I stink?"

"Cigarettes," she said, trying for cool, distant, and intimidating, like him.

"Well... you payin'." He pushed the open-Sesame button.

Paying! She was paying! That was the key to everything. Before, somebody else was always paying — paying was the power she'd never had. This could be a fun trip after all.

"You mind taking me to Houma instead of Lockport?"

"That'll cost you another ten bucks."

"Of course." And she gave him a big smile, deciding she could be nice if it was her choice. Also, she found it made her feel... adult. But maybe that was just the unaccustomed sensation of being in charge.

To her surprise, Lamar returned the smile. "And you ain' gon' tell my uncle, right?"

"Never!" She was enjoying this feeling.

"Well, okay then."

She asked him to drop her at the bookstore, and as she got out, she thanked him, but she didn't get a third smile. "No problem," he said, and peeled off. Okay, then. Not gonna miss you.

She took a moment to adjust. She was back in her hometown. Her mother was here, but Delaney Thibodeaux was the last person she wanted to see. She wished her mother a horrible death. She'd spent the last two years wishing that.

It was a 30-minute walk to Maw-Maw's house, about a mile and a half. She wanted to get some better clothes, at least some clean jeans, to come home in, but she couldn't wait. She felt jumpy, and kind of like her brain itched, but in a good way, like she was on pills. It was that feeling you got when something good was going to happen. Like when Santa Claus came or you got to go to a fair.

8

S kip had the second shift, but she was going in early, jonesing to get back to the Short-Term Murder case. Damn Steve for naming it that! She couldn't get it out of her head. She was driving to work at about 10:15, refreshed by a decent night's sleep, when she heard the little text chirp. "In a minute," she thought, and then the phone rang. "Later, okay?" It rang again.

"Okay, okay," she told it, pulling over to wrestle the device out of her pocket. Abasolo. This had to be good — she was about to see him in ten minutes.

"What's up, A.A.?"

"Where are you?"

"On my way in. You want to know what I'm wearing too?

"Meet me at the Buy-me."

"Very funny. You're at the Bayou, I presume?" A fleabag motel where you could get just about any illegal substance or variety of sex you wanted. Her heart speeded up. This was something big. And nothing good; she'd been wrong about that.

"You will not believe the case I just caught."

"Aww, hell. I've got a bad feeling."

"Trust that instinct."

It was Miguel Bustamente. He was still lying fully clothed on a rumpled bed, a syringe falling out of his elbow pit.

"Coroner's on the way," Abasolo said. "But not much doubt about the cause of death."

"Damn. I should have gone to that bar last night."

"Don't worry about it — from the looks of him, he wasn't there, either."

"Aww, hell, Miguel," she said. "You got a nerve doing this just when I needed you."

"Maybe he didn't do it. Look at the rest of the room."

The place was a wreck — or as much of a wreck as a minimal motel room could be. There wasn't a lot to destroy. But a bedside table and lamp had been knocked over, the bulb broken, everything else on the surface spilled on the floor, although that was nothing much — just a phone, charger, and box of tissues. The television was out of whack, as if someone had hit it, causing it to misalign itself. Cups — both paper and crockery — littered the floor, clearly thrown or swept off of something.

Skip said, "Looks like someone had a fight."

"Yeah."

"I already took a look around," A.A. said. "The fight could have been a robbery — no money, no drugs, no phone. But..."

"Yeah. If Miguel had enough heroin to o.d., why didn't the thief take that?"

And then Read arrived: "We have to stop meeting like this." With a little wink at Abasolo. The coroner wasn't far behind, so they went out to canvass. The results: Yes, there had been a fight. People had heard things. But no, no one had investigated and double no, nobody'd seen nothin'.

"Wonder if there's a Mrs. Bustamente?" Abasolo wondered glumly and went off to follow the various Texas leads, leaving Skip pondering where to go next on Benny's case.

It had to be Dustin, she decided, if her suspect was Benny's customer. She gave him a call. "Had a chance to look up who your Airbnb tenant was?"

"No disrespect, Sergeant, but are you trying to get me to do your job for you?"

"You know," Skip said, "let's don't do this on the phone. I'll be right over." She hung up on him.

Dustin-and-Mom lived in an Irish Channel shotgun, the kind that was rapidly getting rehabbed and repurposed, but theirs was the real thing, right down to the metal awnings from the '50s. Mrs. De Blanc was built for comfort, not speed, as she announced to explain her slow progress through the house, sporting a short gray hairdo with plenty of curls and a T-shirt over cotton pants that were either cropped or too short. Skip thought the latter.

Dustin was as lovely as advertised by Bette from the vintage shop. And as slick as he sounded. He was tall and dark, with Cajun good looks, shaved arms and, she supposed, a shaved chest and legs as well. His face was abloom with health and roses, his biceps and shoulders bursting merrily from his olive tank top.

By way of greeting, he said, "Well, aren't you a tall one."

"Yeah. You don't want to mess with me." She smiled when she said it, but she said it tough enough to send the message. "Got that contract?"

Not surprisingly, he did. The customer was an Adam George from Houston, and he had paid by credit card.

"Did you see him? Talk to him?"

"That's not how it works. They just book online. You know this is going to ruin my business, don't you?"

"I thought your landlord closed you down."

"Oh, he did. The fucker. I meant the studio."

"Really? You're having yoga dropouts?"

"If it gets out about what that perv painted on the wall, I will."

"You really think so? You could always change the studio name."

"I already did that. We used to be Namaste World, but I found this web series called Namaste Bitch and I kind of stole that. And then everybody wanted to take yoga!"

"I thought you might have stolen that."

"You know that series?"

"Since yesterday."

"Well, anyway, can you keep this out of the press?"

"The writing on the wall? Definitely. And I'd appreciate it if you'd keep it quiet too."

"You're a little bit late with that. I bet I've told fifty people."

Skip gave him her Mean Cop look. "Well. You can't have it both ways, Dustin. But it might help us catch this guy if you could keep it quiet."

"You know what the worst part is? Now I've lost my income stream. And I have to live in that place. It's been defiled!"

"Burn some sage," she said. "Everything'll be fine. Oh, hey, tell you what — I know some witches who could do a banishing for you." Maybe they could banish Dustin while they were at it.

"Well, aren't you Miss Full-Service Cop."

~

ADAM GEORGE. Well, great. Here goes nothing, she thought as she began her search.

And nothing it was. There was no Adam George at that address in Houston. And no Adam George in Houston at all. Okay, then. No surprise, fake ID. Who uses their own credit card to rent a crime scene?

That was the end of the easy part. She was going to have find that hooker. She called Abasolo: "A.A., you want to get lunch?"

"Definitely. I have stuff for you. Joey K's?"

"No way! Let's do the Red Dog. They have salads."

"I said I have stuff for you."

"I stand corrected. Joey K's in 20."

If Miguel had to go and off himself, she thought, the good news was she and Abasolo were practically partners on both cases. And she couldn't think of a better partner. Even if he was making her eat at Joey K's.

It was a perfectly fine old-style neighborhood restaurant — that was why he liked it — but they were much more noted for their fried delights than their green ones. She'd weigh a thousand pounds if she actually ate that stuff, while A.A., who always ate their fried food, never gained a pound.

He was already waiting at one of the no-frills, no-cloth tables. "Hmmm... the fried chicken or the red beans and rice?"

"Maybe I could get a veggie plate."

"You're no fun."

"Yes, but I'm buying. Was there a Mrs. Bustamente?"

"If so, I don't know why she'd want to claim him. Miguel's got quite a little rap sheet."

"Surprise!"

"Well, he's not just any pimp. He's involved with a big ol' human trafficking operation."

"Awww, hell!" Skip was thinking of the video footage from the umbrella store. Come to think of it, the woman had been very slight — more like a girl than a woman. "Tell me we're not looking for a minor."

A minor who might have been kidnapped by a freak.

"See, good thing we didn't go to the Red Dog. You're not going to be able to eat, so what does it matter?"

"Wrong, I can always eat. Listen, we've gotta find this girl. Are you thinking what I'm thinking?"

"That maybe the perp's got her? Wannabe serial killer gets sidewise with her pimp, kills him, and then kidnaps her? Yeah." He quit eating his fried chicken and gave her a take-no-prisoners look. "It's crossed my mind."

"And then her other pimp dies after a fight — coincidence?"

"The killer could be covering his tracks."

"But what if she got away? We've got to cover that base too."

"Actually, if she's a minor, that could work for us. There aren't that many places she can go. Why don't you try Melody?"

"Melody! Great idea." Melody Brocato was someone Skip had met on a case, as a 16-year-old runaway musician. She now had a day gig at a runaway shelter and by night rocked out with three different bands, including her own. "You get anything else out of Houston P.D.?"

"Yeah. Miguel's got a 'known associate'. Did a lot of business with another pimp — guy named Lloyd Handler. I asked them to pick him up for questioning."

"Did you ask him about the missing girl?"

"The informant didn't know anything specific. She could

be Mexican, or Honduran, or ... anything. It would curl your hair, the ways they get these girls."

"So what you're saying is there are a lot of them — and they're disposable and nobody can keep track of them."

A.A. gave her a look like *Yeah, and you know it too.* They both knew the statistics — trafficking victims had a shockingly short average lifespan. Neither said anything, spontaneously observing a simultaneous moment of silence.

Finally Skip broke it. "Okay, let's get the bill. I've got to get back to the office."

She was itching to get to Melody. And she had an idea.

Cody got a bad feeling when she saw the place. It was Maw-Maw's house, but not really. It used to be white but all dirty, with metal awnings, overgrown flowerbeds, and a yard full of leaves and little pine-cone things with red seeds from her magnolia tree.

The magnolia was still there, but the grass was pristine, and there were different plants in the beds, neat well-kept ones. Even more telling — the ancient awnings were gone and the house had been painted, a pretty blue door added. Unless Maw-Maw had won the lottery, well... Cody's heart thumped with fear.

Summoning every ounce of moxie Terry had always told her she had, she knocked on the door. A girl about her own age answered, a blonde with a ponytail and jeans that fit her like shrink wrap. "Hi, my grandma used to live here? I guess she's moved?"

"We've been here over a year," the girl said.

"Do you... uh... do you know where she is?"

"No, sorry."

"She didn't... uh... didn't...?" Cody couldn't bring herself to say the word "die".

Apparently catching on that it was pretty weird not to know where your own grandmother was — even whether was alive or dead — the girl froze up. "I'm sorry. I can't help you." She shut the door.

Now Cody was mad. She leaned on the bell till she finally got a shouted, "Go away! My mom's not home."

Sure enough, there was no car in the driveway. Well, she could wait till the mom came home, but she noticed that the house next door looked exactly as it always had. She couldn't quite remember the family's name — wait! It was Blanchard. Might be anyway. Good enough. She cut across the lawn.

Mrs. Blanchard was wearing an apron, like some cookie-baking maw-maw in a commercial, and that fact alone made Cody's knees weak. She had once been part of this world. She didn't know if she could ever get it back.

"Cordelia?" Mrs. Blanchard said. "Can it be... little Cordelia? With pink hair?"

"Hi, Mrs. Blanchard."

Mrs. Blanchard grabbed her, hugged her way too hard. Cody was mystified. She barely knew the woman. "We thought you were dead."

Cody hadn't thought of that. Well, who knew what story her mother had told, but everyone knew her mother and probably no one believed it, whatever it was. She said, "I'm fine. I've just been away."

"Your grandmother's missed you so much!"

"Is she... okay?" It came out barely a whisper.

"Oh, you poor child, you don't even know? Where have you been?"

"Maw-Maw died?" This time Cody managed to say the

word and to her surprise didn't die herself just because her lips formed it. She realized she'd been kind of expecting to. But her heart picked up speed and her entire muscle structure clenched as she braced for the answer.

"Oh, no, she's fine! She's great! She just moved over to St. Anthony's Gardens. She loves it there. It's a retirement home, baby. She's very happy there."

A new fear gripped her. "Does she have Alzheimer's?"

"Oh, no, dawlin'." Mrs. Blanchard winked. "I think she has a boy friend."

"A what?" Cody felt like she'd been punched.

"What's wrong with me?" Mrs. Blanchard untied the sash of her apron. "Come on in, my baby. Ya hungry?"

"Oh, no, thanks. But if you could give me directions to St. Anthony's Gardens, I'd really appreciate it." Listen to me, she thought, talking just like a normal person, polite and everything. Like nothing ever changed.

"I'm not giving you directions, I'm takin' you there right now!"

Cody felt her face break out in smiles. Great big unstoppable smiles she really couldn't control. To her embarrassment, she felt hot tears on her cheeks as well. "You are?"

They didn't even stop to phone or text. But once whisked into the car, Cody got quite a few more questions than she'd bargained for. Where had she been? What had she been doing? What grade was she in now?

She absolutely wasn't prepared. She'd been with her other grandmother, she said, (although she didn't even know who her father was, much less his mother). And she'd just been going to school, nothing much else. She thought of other lies — she wanted to say she'd gotten a part in the school play, maybe an A in science, but when she thought those kinds of things, even before she tried to say them, she felt her throat closing and knew her voice would break. They were all the things she hadn't done and hadn't thought about for so long. It hurt so much to think about her life before Miguel.

The fourteen-year-old Cody hated her life — her crazy drugged-out mom, never having nice clothes like the other kids, never being able to afford anything, even school supplies, not having a real home, only a trailer, not having a dad, never being able to have anyone over — boy, she couldn't complain enough. She'd had friends, though. And school — she actually liked school. Did anyone like school? Cody did. It was so much better than home. She also knew that one day she'd grow up and be able to get away.

And then all of a sudden every piece of it was gone and she ached with loss if she let herself think about it. She would gladly have parted with a limb to get any part of it back — and that wasn't just a figure of speech. She would have. All except for her mother. She never wanted to see that bitch again.

The "senior residence" wasn't what Cody expected. She'd seen those tiny nursing homes that looked like motels, but this was a whole different animal. A high-rise, for Houma. It looked like a city apartment building, only it had a little marquee of sorts — announcing its name — and a circular driveway like a hotel.

"I think I better go tell her first," Blanchard said. "We don't want her having a heart attack."

But Cody couldn't wait, not one second longer. She opened the car door and left it that way, flinging herself through the entrance and nearly knocking over a lady with a walker. People were sitting in what looked like an ordinary living room, only bigger, but there was a tiny office at the entrance. "I'm here for Chantelle Thibodeaux," she said, prompting someone in the living room to rise, a woman with her back to Cody. And then the woman turned around.

"Maw-Maw," Cody said, "it's me." She spoke in a whisper, unable to coax out any more sound, but that was okay. Maw-Maw ran to her — or rather ran partway to her, since she had quite a limp now, her arthritis having apparently gotten worse. Cody made up the distance, and they hugged hard enough to leave bruises.

Maw-Maw was crying, outright bawling, repeating the same words over and over, "My baby's come home, my baby's alive, oh thank God, thank God, thank God, my baby's come home."

Cody, for her part, couldn't speak, could only gasp and make hideous guttural noises she didn't recognize as sobs, only as attempts to get some air in her lungs, start breathing again, get her body to work like it intended to live.

"Turn around, y'all." For some reason both obeyed, and there was Mrs. Blanchard beaming and snapping their picture.

That brought Cody around. "Wait! You can't do that! Please don't take my picture."

"Baby, what's wrong? It's not like you're wanted by the police or something."

She hoped her face didn't give her away. She looked her grandmother square in the eye. "Maw-Maw. I've had a really horrible time."

Instantly, Maw-Maw put her arm around her, drawing her close to her own thick, comforting body. "Josie, ya brought my baby here? You just gave me back my life, dawlin'." She left Cody and went to hug the other woman, and as she did, Cody saw her whisper something. She said aloud, "Really, I just... I don't know how to thank you."

Josie beamed some more. "I was almost as happy to see her as you were. I'm gon' leave you two alone now."

"I just said we'd see about things tomorrow, dawlin'. Asked for a little breathin' space."

Cody didn't buy it. She'd been around liars too long. She knew there was something else.

But she knew her grandmother wasn't going to get to it right away. First she had to tell her story. But how could she tell her grandmother her own daughter had sold her? Instead she wailed out the thing she'd been thinking for the last two years. "Why didn't you look for me?"

"Oh, my poor, poor baby." All she could do for the next five minutes was hold onto Cody and cry. Finally she said, "Dawlin', we looked everywhere for you. I even hired a private detective. But I didn't even know you were gone until... well, I don't know how long... just, one day I talked to your mom and she said you ran away. I called your school and they said you quit. But they made it sound like it was awhile longer ago than your mom did. She said it was a week ago and she didn't tell me 'cause she knew you'd be back. The school said it was about a month ago. Baby, why'd you go and quit school? That just doesn't seem like you."

Cody wanted to cry and scream and jump up and down and howl at the moon. She took a few minutes to collect her thoughts before she spoke. She'd learned this method in the years with Miguel — because if she said the wrong thing she'd be beaten. But it didn't work this time. "You believed my crazy mom?" she hollered.

Her grandmother looked around apologetically. "Let's go outside to talk."

Outside was good. This way they could walk as they talked. This was better for Cody because she found she suddenly had a lot of nervous energy she didn't know how to handle. She was frightened and angry and anxious all at once. And she was happy too, because she was home; and because everything seemed normal, even if it still felt like a dream; and because she was with Maw-Maw. She could just barely catch forgotten glimpses of her old life and maybe even start to imagine life again. She didn't consider herself to have been living the last two years. She'd tried to think of it as serving time in prison, like Malcolm X had, and the Count of Monte Cristo, and Cookie on Empire. Prison was something you got out of, and she knew that, no matter what she had to do to make it happen, she was getting out of The Life, as they called it. It was anything but life. It wasn't just prison but prison with torture. At first when she wouldn't do what they wanted, they beat her, and then when she had to do it to keep from getting beaten, she found ways to make it easier for herself. She tried to engage the customers on a personal level, flirt with them a little, make them laugh, be real sweet to them if they didn't smell bad and were gentle and semi-respectful and didn't make her talk dirty to them. She wanted them to ask for her again, so she didn't have to put up with the gross disgusting ones. But that backfired, in a way — because repeat customers made her an ever more valuable commodity. Miguel needed her more than before, more than he needed some of the other girls.

And so she sucked up. She sucked up big-time, so he'd think he had the happiest little whore in Texas working for him. Because she knew all he had to do was turn his back once and she was outta there. She would silently hum that war song from Sunday school, the one about the Christian soldiers, when she needed to keep her spirits up. Her favorite part was the line that said, "onward as to war!" The "cross of Jesus" part didn't interest her any more. Jesus wasn't anywhere in Texas that she could see — all she had was herself. So she rewrote the line.

> "With the cross of Jesus
> Going on before"

became

> "I will get my life back
> Once I find the door."

That meant the door she was going to walk out of. Only it hadn't been a door — it turned out to be a pole she had to shimmy down — and now she'd killed somebody and so she was probably going to jail.

And yet... now that she was here, out walking in the fresh air with her grandmother, in the town she grew up in, she wasn't a criminal surrounded by criminals any more. Things looked different. She hadn't just killed a man for no reason — she'd killed that man in self-defense, right? Was she really going to prison? Or did she have a chance? She didn't have any perspective anymore, anything or anybody to compare herself to.

Of course she had robbed him. And she'd also robbed her friend, maybe her best friend ever. You could go to prison for that just as easily as murder.

Maw-Maw picked up the conversation where Cody'd left it. "Baby, of course I didn't believe your mom. Nothin' but lies came out of that woman's mouth once she got on them pills. She was so promising too — smart like you with two years of college and everything..." She shook her head and made the universal Southern expression of bewilderment. "Mmm mmm mmm."

"Well, what did you think happened?"

"I thought you ran away, like she said — I would have if she was my mother. I just thought there was more to the story — like maybe you were with a boy. Or pregnant or something. But whatever it was, I knew you didn't have any business being out there on your own. You were barely just fourteen. So I hired me somebody to find you. We just couldn't come up with nothin'."

Cody felt like biting the bark off some trees, just to let off steam. "Why didn't you go to the police?"

"Well. I should have. But... we've never had no police in our family. Nobody goes to the police for any reason! You know? That was the rule. And people told me stuff — they wouldn't do nothin' about a runaway, stuff like that. I couldn't even find out how long you'd been gone. And I didn't want to get you in no trouble."

"Trouble? What kind of trouble would I be in?"

"Well, baby, I didn't know what you might have done. You could have been sellin' drugs like ya mama, for all I knew!" Her grandmother stopped talking and faced her, her face full of anguish. "Baby, if you were gon' run away, why wouldn't you run to me? I would have taken care of you."

Cody thought she was going to have a heart attack herself. Her heart was about to leap out of her chest, and she could hardly breathe. "I have to sit down," she said. And she did, right on the curb.

"Maw-Maw," she said, between deep breaths, "I might have some kinda bad news to tell you."

"Oh, baby!" Maw-Maw started to cry. "I got some for you too!"

S kip's idea was to see if she could get a decent image from that scrap of video from the umbrella store. She thought an artist might be able to come up with a reasonable guess as to what the girl with the pink-tipped hair actually looked like. She copied it to her phone and headed out to see Stella Brundage, the artist the department most often used for sketching suspects — when they could get her. Stella was a remarkably talented portrait painter and nobody's idea of a police artist. They'd discovered her by accident — on her own case. She was able to draw her own mugger so perfectly a neighbor had recognized him, and they talked her into working for the department. But she hated coming to headquarters.

Skip was always a little intimidated by her house, a mansion by any standards and a very formal one, the sort of place where portraits by famous portrait painters actually hung. It was full of them, but mostly not Stella's, mostly paintings dating back to the days when Stella's ancestors had first come to Louisiana.

Fortunately Stella's studio, an outbuilding behind the

house, where most of her neighbors had swimming pools, was its polar opposite, flooded with light and clutter. Skip was shown there by a maid wearing a uniform that could have come from the 1950s.

"Hey, Skip. Glad you came over. I could use a break." Somebody should really do her portrait, Skip thought as Stella stepped into the garden. She was an imposing figure of the sort she thought she'd never be herself, despite her six feet of height. Stella wasn't as tall, but she had a trick of posture or carriage that made her look as if you ought to obey her. Even when dressed as she was now, in floppy-legged old canvas pants and an oversized paint-stained shirt, hair escaping from its loose twist. But what hair! Jet black with a three-inch-wide streak of white in the front, which she swore was natural. Anyone else would have looked like a skunk; Stella looked like the queen of Uptown.

Skip said, "Got an unorthodox request for you. Here's some video we got the other day." Stella stared at it as if it were matter from an unknown planet.

"The man's dead and the girl's a witness. He's a pimp and suspected human trafficker. We think she was his victim, but somehow she got away and she's still out there, maybe with no place to go. I'm trying to find her for information, but I'm not going to lie, I'm also worried about her — for a variety of hair-raising reasons.

"I want to see if I can find anyone who's seen her. Think you can do anything with that profile? It's all I've got. Wait, except for some hairs. They're dark, long, thick and curly. With pink tips."

"Oh, yeah, that bottom-color thing. What do you call that?"

Skip laughed. "Been trying to remember for days."

Stella was staring at the picture. "Too bad it's too dark to see her skin color — but I'm thinking Latina. What do you think?"

Skip stared at it again. "I just... can't tell." The truth was she couldn't tell much at all. She was beginning to think this was a fool's errand.

"Give me a couple of hours," Stella said.

"Really? You think you can get something?"

She nodded "I've got some ideas. Want me to text you?"

"Sure. Terrific!" Skip was almost elated. "I really didn't expect anything."

She trudged back through the gloomy mausoleum Stella called a house and wondered how such a vibrant woman could stand to live there — probably something to do with a husband who thought it represented his place in the world. Outside, she checked for missed texts and calls and saw Abasolo's "Call me."

"Got something good," he said. "The Houston guys couldn't find Handler, but they talked to an informant he works with. Seems he and Miguel brought a load of girls to the Sugar Bowl, then Handler brought the girls back."

"So?"

"Then he left again. Said he had to help Miguel with something."

"He's back here?"

"It would seem so. What do you bet the 'something's' bringing in Pinky?"

"Oooh. Hate that idea."

"Yeah, but the good news is we might be able to find him. I've got a mug shot. Want to take a ride out to the Buy-me?"

"I'll meet you there."

Today's motel desk clerk was Troy Johnson, a young black man who was incongruously clean-cut, polite, and as it turned out, even helpful. Skip wanted to bundle him up and get him out of there. After introductions, she said, "You like your job?" and he laughed.

"I go to UNO and all my friends have jobs, you know? Guess who makes the most money? Me. The person with the worst job in town! They almost can't pay anybody to do this — meaning anybody who won't steal 'em blind or nod out on China White they got from one of the... uh... guests. They could make one of their kids do it, but who wants their kids around this shit? So they pay really well. Somebody's gotta do it, you know?"

"Good attitude," she said.

"'Course it does require some going blind or deaf now and then... but I don't know anything about that murder yesterday."

Abasolo said, "We're not here to bust you for anything. We just need a little help." He produced the picture. "Have you seen this guy?"

"Oh, yeah. He's here right now. Probably in his room."

Lloyd was there, all right, and from the smell of the place — alcohol, pot, and unwashed human — he had been ever since he got back from Houston. He came to the door in nothing but a pair of ancient jeans riding way too low on his scraggly frame, his hair looking as if he'd poured motor oil on it, his cheeks unshaved, unkempt, and grayish.

He seemed to take their badges pretty much in stride. "Thish about Miguel?" he managed to slur. "I don't know nothin'."

He tried to slam the door, but Abasolo had his foot wedged in the doorway.

"Hey, look," Skip said. "Isn't that pot over there? Right in plain sight?"

They pushed him aside and seized the pot. A.A. said,

"Looks like you're going to get some sober-up time in our luxurious new jail. You'll love it, it's practically a resort."

WHEN THEY HAD him in an interview room, they started in the middle. "Why'd you kill Miguel, Lloyd?"

"Didn't kill him. Know what happened, though. The whale killed him. Man, this thing's messed up! Benny bought it too. Then Miguel gets it. And Cody's missin'. She's probably as dead as they are. I'm gonna be next, you know? The guy's a psycho!"

Skip said, "You want to start from the beginning?"

"I don't know, man. I don't even know where to start."

"Well, for openers, who's the whale?"

"See, I don't even know that. I don't even know if Miguel knew. I'm damned sure Benny didn't know."

"Well, let's try what, then. What's a whale, to you?"

He put his elbows on the table and tucked his face into his open palms. Thinking, maybe. Finally he straightened up.

"If I tell you, what do I get out of this?"

Oh, man, do you need a lawyer! Skip thought. But it wasn't her place to tell him — and it was also the last thing she wanted to do.

She said, "I think you killed your buddy, Lloyd. So... life, if you're lucky. Maybe the needle. We have lethal injection in Louisiana, you know that? They say it's the most humane way."

"I didn't kill nobody!"

"You convince me of that, and then we'll talk. What about the whale?"

He gave her a long, desperate stare that managed

somehow to be sullen and despairing at the same time. Finally he blurted, "Fuck it! Either I get the needle or the whale gets me — ain't no way I can win in this thing!"

"We can protect you. I can promise you that."

"No, you can't. Nobody can." But Skip could see she'd won — so long as he didn't ask for a lawyer. She waited.

Finally, he said. "Biggest one-time score we'd had in a long time. This guy was offering some serious bucks."

"To do what?"

"We had to get him a girl — black-Latin mix, he wanted. He didn't care about the age, but Cody was all we had. And we had to rent a place on Airbnb and take her there. That was all. For $2000. Now that's a whale!"

"That was for all night?"

"Yeah. Usually goes for about $500. And he paid for the room too."

"How'd you make the deal?"

"It was slick as snot, man. We just did it online. We ran an ad for girls at the Sugar Bowl. He found us, paid half in advance by credit card. Supposed to give Benny the rest when he delivered her. Goddammit, Benny didn't know his ass! Miguel shoulda gone himself. But we had this whole string of girls, ya know? Somebody had to do the wranglin'."

"Did Benny collect the money?"

"Yeah, man! He texted us. Easiest money we ever made." He stopped to consider. "Except we didn't. The whale musta taken it back when he killed Benny — hey, did Benny have any money on him?"

Now that she thought about it, he didn't. "Why would he kill Benny?" she said.

He held two fingers up, as if he had a cigarette between them. "See, I thought about that. I thought maybe something to do with Cody. Maybe she wouldn't do what he wanted, something like that. Maybe she..."

"Maybe she what?"

He face-palmed again, and again came up with the sullen-desperate look. "She's gone, see? We don't know where she is."

Abasolo said, "Who's we, Lloyd?"

"Me and Miguel. That's all."

"So why do you think he killed Miguel?"

"'Cause I heard a fight in there, man! Somebody killed Miguel!"

Skip said, "You heard the fight? So did you investigate?"

"Hell, no, I didn't! You don't go investigating things at the Buy-Me."

"You telling me you heard somebody attacking your buddy and business partner and you couldn't be bothered trying to help him?"

He shrugged. "I was wasted."

That I can believe, Skip thought. She said, "So what's the deal with Cody?"

He almost brightened at that. "Man, now that's a mystery. Benny didn't come outta that door and neither did Cody. The Whale mighta killed her too. We don't know what the hell happened to her — tha's why I'm still here. We were lookin' for her."

"You think she got away, don't you?"

He shrugged. "She's a free agent."

"We don't think she is," Abasolo said. "You kidnapped her, didn't you? She's just a kid!" He was furious and letting it show. Skip thought he'd gone too far.

Lloyd raised his voice. "Hey, man, I'm helping you. You asked me to help you out with Miguel's murder. I done that, okay? You don't know what you're talking about."

"All you said was you heard a fight — that's all you got? You gotta give us something, Lloyd."

"I don't know nothin'."

"Let's start with the girl, okay?" Skip said softly, hoping she sounded non-threatening. This was the part that mattered. "Who is she?"

"I don't know. Somebody Miguel knows. He calls her Cody. Tha's all I fuckin' know!"

"You said 'we'."

"What?"

"Earlier. You talked about the whale wanting a certain kind of girl and you said 'Cody's all we had'."

"Yeah, right. Miguel knew a girl he thought could do the job."

"How old is she, Lloyd?"

"How should I know? Young! Twenty, twenty-one, I guess. What the hell is this?"

Abasolo said, "Twenty-one, my ass."

Skip's phone vibrated. She said, "We'll get back to you, Lloyd," and checked for messages. "Oh. My. God. Look at that."

"Look at what?" Abasolo asked.

But she held up the screen to Lloyd. "Know this girl?"

"Shit! How'd you get that?"

"Who is she?"

"It's Cody, goddammit. You know goddam well it's Cody. Where is she? She dead or what?"

"Like I said. We'll get back to you."

As soon as they were alone, she showed Abasolo the drawing Stella had sent. "Look what Stella did." It was a very detailed police-style portrait of a teen-age girl with wild curly hair, drawn in black as usual, but plainly showing pink on the ends.

"Impressive. How'd she do it?"

"Who knows? Swear to god she's a magician. All she had was that little video clip and the word 'curly'."

"What? You didn't give her 'balayage'?"

"That's it! The color thing — you Googled it, you rat!"

He shrugged. "Well, you could have done it yourself. So... who is this girl? Ethnically speaking."

"She's from Houston, so she could be Hispanic. But if she were from here, I'd say maybe African-American."

"Or white," Abasolo said.

"Yeah. I kind of get what Lloyd meant when he said she was what the freak ordered up."

"Speaking of which... the freak!"

"Yeah, the whale. But Cody's our best lead to him. Hey, cheer up. We've got a picture and a name. How about we run this over to McAvoy and see if he can get it on nola.com?"

"You know he can. McAvoy can get ink if we so much as give out a parking ticket."

"Such is the digital world. It may not be him so much as that every news site is now a voracious animal that eats press releases like peanuts. Don't you find yourself checking news sites several times a day?"

"Guilty," the sergeant said. "But sheepish about it. You know... this could be a major trafficking ring."

"Houston said no. Just these two guys."

"So why weren't they in jail if the cops knew all about them?"

"Really good question. Who's with the girls now?"

"Yeah. It's gotta be more than these two."

"Let's revisit that little issue with Lloyd next time we talk to him."

"Come on, let's get to McAvoy. I've got a bad feeling about Cody."

"Yeah. Me too, and I've been trying to shake it. What if he's got her?"

"You know what."

Skip didn't answer. If the whale had her, he'd probably already killed her.

10

C ody just blurted it. She didn't think she could do it any other way. "Mama sold me to a pimp."

She knew her grandmother was going to take it hard, but the howl she let out was so intense people were looking out their windows to see who was hurt.

"And then he sold me to another pimp, who took me to Texas. Maw-Maw, they watched me every minute. And they beat me if I didn't... you know..."

Maw-Maw put her arms around Cody's shoulders and hugged the girl's head to her soft, comforting breasts, holding her way too tight, as if someone was trying to tear her away.

"Baby baby baby baby baby," was all she said, over and over again. And both of them sobbed like they'd been needing to every day for the past year, maybe in Cody's case her whole life. Maw-Maw said, "I wish I'd known, I wish I'd known..." but Cody didn't think anyone could have found her. Miguel always destroyed everyone's I.D., never used last names, and gave everyone new first names to use with the clients. Cody's was Lola.

She used to wonder if she'd ended up on a milk carton — and then she'd wonder if anyone had ever been found that way.

She said, as gently as she could, "Maw-Maw, I'm okay. Look at me. I'm in one piece."

But that just started up the crying engine again, Cody wasn't sure why. When she was cried out, Maw-Maw pulled herself together — Cody could almost see her doing it — and said, "Let's walk some more." And as they walked, Maw-Maw unfurled her own bad news. "Cordelia, honey, I'm pretty sure your mama was real, real sorry for what she did."

Cody sniffed, thinking, like I care. She said, "I'm sure she was. As soon as she spent the $5000, and needed more."

"Are you ready for that bad news I mentioned?" Without waiting for an answer, Maw-Maw said, "She's dead, honey. She o.d.'d right after that time we talked about you. I always knew she wouldn't have anything to live for without you, but I sure didn't know she had to live with knowing she'd done something a... an animal wouldn't do!"

Cody was trying to take it in. Her mother... dead? Cody'd thought she'd always be there, hovering, frightening, and shaming her. She didn't know how to take this, but much as she'd wished her mother dead a million times, she was surprised that the news made her a little sad. You should be sad for your mother, right? She knew that, but the news was also kind of a relief — one less awful thing in her life.

"At the time I thought maybe she'd done it on purpose," said Maw-Maw. "She couldn't have lived as long as she did without knowing you can't mix alcohol and pills."

"And now you don't think so?"

"Now I'm sure she did. Mmm. Mmm. Mmm. What a terrible burden to bear!"

Cody gave her the side-eye, feeling less and less sad as

the conversation went on. "Yeah, well. Excuse me if I don't feel sorry for her."

And that set Maw-Maw off again. Cody hadn't considered how it might affect her. "Aw, Maw-Maw, why are you crying? I'm so sorry. I wouldn't make you cry for anything."

"I know you wouldn't, dawlin'. You know what we gotta do? We've gotta figure out what we're gonna do next. You have any clothes with you?"

"No, ma'am. I... well, I'm not kidding when I say I ran away. I had to go out the back way and slide down a pole from the second floor."

"Well, first let's get you some clothes. Let's go back and get my car and you can tell me how you got away while we shop. I'm wonderin'..." She frowned and chewed her lip.

Cody didn't like the look of it. "What, Maw-Maw?"

"Baby. You been trafficked — what happened to you just idn't something we can forget about. I gotta tell you something." Her gentle face went all hard and stiff. "Anybody that hurt you? I ain' gon' rest till their ass is either dead or in jail for the duration. You hear me? I hate to say it, but I think we gotta break the no-police rule on this one."

Cody was silent. Even in her agitated state, she could see that this was going to happen eventually. She couldn't run her whole life. And she had nowhere to run anyway — she was already there. She had to confess to killing the customer and take whatever was coming. She could do that. She might go to prison, but if she did, it couldn't be half as bad as what she'd already suffered. And somehow, out here, she was thinking more and more that a 16-year-old sex slave who killed a customer she thought was about to kill her was going to be listened to, not just dismissed as... nobody. Because nobody was who she'd been for the past two years. A nobody who slept in a barracks in a falling-down house with seven other nobodies, always guarded, always kept in the dark— literally. Miguel had blackout shades over all the windows and never let the girls turn on the lights in the daytime or have phones or computers or any contact with anyone but each other and customers. They had television, but weren't allowed to watch the news.

Maw-Maw gave her shoulder a little squeeze. "Not today, baby. No way. You deserve a day or two of peace and quiet."

"Really?" Could she have heard right? A day or two in which she didn't have to have sex with multiple disgusting men or else run for her life? "Maw-Maw, could I really have that?"

"Awwww, baby." Maw-Maw's eyes went wet again. Cody'd never known she was so emotional.

Cody was wondering where she was going to stay, though. She'd assumed she could stay with Maw-Maw. But did they let teen-agers stay in senior houses? Somehow, she thought not. But her grandmother surprised her.

"We've got a guest room at St. Anthony's. How would you like to spend the night with a hundred folks about a hundred years old?"

"That sounds as good as the Waldorf-Astoria!" For the first time she made her grandmother laugh. But Maw-Maw had said "spend the night", as if it was a one-time thing. What would happen after that?

"What are you hungry for? Tonight we're goin' out on the town."

"I'm actually kinda hungry now."

Cody let her grandmother buy her the best grilled cheese anyone ever tasted, and then some jeans, T-shirts, and underwear, even a pair of pajamas. She didn't know how to explain that she had plenty of money, but it was stolen from a dead man and her best friend. She wished she had the courage to ask for a phone but thought she could take care of that later, when she had some time alone.

When she was settled at St. Anthony's, she felt almost giddy, as if she really were at the Waldorf. There was a TV in her room — her own TV! — and a library downstairs with all the books you could want and a computer she could use. Her grandmother had told her so. She even had the wi-fi password. She almost had to pinch herself.

Right now the shower and plush towels beckoned, and after that the prospect of a nap on a real bed that wasn't a bunk — an actual queen-sized bed with soft sheets instead of a dirty, scratchy old blanket. She slept the sleep of the dead.

When she woke up, everything was dark. According to the bedside clock it was 1:10 a.m. She'd missed out on the dinner Maw-Maw had promised. She closed her eyes again.

STEVE HAD CALLED to say there was no need to pick Rambla up, the whole Scoggin-Ritter family was coming over for an impromptu barbecue.

"Barbecue? It's January."

"Yes, but did you ever see a more beautiful day?"

It was like early April. "Come to think of it, no. What's the occasion?"

"Your copy of Martha Stewart Magazine came and..."

"I do not subscribe to Martha Stewart Magazine!"

"Well, they send it anyway. Food and Wine too. Anyhow, there's this Asian salmon thing I want to do. Kenny's bringing a date and Sheila's bringing Rambla home."

It was too dark to eat outside — though really not too cool, even after sundown — so Steve had set their long farm table using dish towels as place mats. Oooooh, I love this domestic thing, Skip thought. Maybe he's Martha Stewart.

Which was exactly the joke Jimmy Dee made when he saw it. Just like old times. Except that the kids were grown up. Sheila was predictably beautiful, feisty, and opinionated, and Kenny'd discovered a musical side, which perfectly fed his already unconventional tendencies, brought on, Jimmy Dee thought, by the peer stresses of living with two gay uncles.

Tonight he'd brought a girl friend who had the unkempt look of a gutterpunk, the seasonal transients who blew into town in the winter — and one ten years older than he was. He'd loaded up on the piercings and tattoos in the last few years, and the girl — a percussionist named Washboard Kiki — was sporting as much ink as he did. Skip thought she looked like the kind of person who'd rip out a sensitive kid's heart and stomp on it. She told herself to reserve judgment, but she could tell Jimmy Dee didn't like her either. He kept calling her "Washboard." Not even "Washboard, darlin'."

She could see Kenny was uncomfortable and eager to impress his date and wondered what she could do to help him. Rambla was usually a great icebreaker, but the minute Sheila walked in with her, she started barking at Kiki.

Kenny gave it a shot himself. "Hey, Aunt Skip, weren't you on that yoga murder? The Airbnb thing?"

"That was me. Murder on Magazine Street — doesn't happen every day."

"Oh, at Namaste Bitch?" Kiki said. "I do restorative there. Dustin's been burning enough sage in there to set off the smoke alarms. He's all broken up about it — or maybe about his business being closed while you guys finish up in there."

"You're a pal of his?" Skip asked.

"Oh, no, I have a different teacher — she's the one who told me. I used to love Dustin, but we fell out over the Airbnb thing. I live in the Marigny and half my neighbors are gone— moved back home, in with their siblings or best friends... now I've got wall-to-wall revelers. Except for this one guy — he bought the double next door and I found out he owns five other single-home Airbnb hotels."

"Hotels?" asked Jimmy Dee.

"Well, that's what they are. Illegal hotels."

Skip was starting to like her. If she'd known neighbors who'd moved out, she was no transient.

Steve said, "Could you introduce me to this guy?"

"Not too sure. He lives in Texas. This is delicious, by the way. Did Kenny tell you I've got a little restaurant in the Marigny? I'd love to get something like this on the menu."

"Well..." Steve looked sheepish. "It's in this month's issue of Martha Stewart Magazine."

"I knew it," Jimmy Dee hollered. Even Layne smirked.

Sheila said, "You're a chef? We thought you were a musician."

"Naaah. Not a chef, just an investor. I'm putting together a house band — we want Kenny to be in it. That's how we met." And she looked at him with such naked affection that Skip mentally tossed her first impressions.

"About that guy in Texas," Steve insisted. "You know his name?"

"I want it too," Sheila said. "We're putting together some pro bono cases involving illegal short-term rentals, and this guy sounds like a serial offender. I want to see if he's one of the defendants."

Kenny said, "People are always talking about it like it's

something they need to... you know... pay the mortgage. Isn't there something wrong with that?"

"Big time," Sheila said.

"Sometimes I don't know if people even realize it's illegal..."

"Well, it's not so illegal as it used to be. Only entire homes, after a certain number of days. Actually, it's a pretty weak law, except in the French Quarter. Other cities have stronger ones."

"Yeah." Steve looked like he was somewhere else. "Yeah. San Francisco; Austin... hey, New York!"

Layne looked at Skip as if only she could restore sanity. "What's up with him?"

"I think," she said, "he just had an idea." Her phone vibrated. "Will you excuse me a moment? Got a phone call."

It was Abasolo, with terrible news.

She returned long enough to say, "Sorry, guys. Gotta go."

"Sit down, presh," Jimmy Dee said. "You look like you're about to faint."

"I'll be okay," she said, grabbing her purse. It was where she kept her weapon.

11

"CoCo, got a surprise for you." Maw-Maw stood as Cody came to breakfast and found her table, as instructed. "Two, if you count Zachary." She gave her granddaughter that quick parental check even Cody's mom used to do. "You look cute in your new jeans."

"Morning, Maw-Maw." Cody sat down at the table and surveyed a sea of white heads, with one orange one and one that was only half-white. Evidently only one person at St. Anthony's believed in hair color — the redhead. The salt-and-pepper guy was natural, she'd be willing to bet.

As if he heard her thinking about him, he stood and made his long, lanky way to their table. Maw-Maw lit up like a star. "Cordelia, meet Zachary Granger. Zachary, this is my beautiful granddaughter." Her eyes glistened. Cody remembered Mrs. Blanchard's remark about a boy friend and thought this might be an important moment for Maw-Maw. Wanting to make it into a ceremony, she stood up and shook the man's hand, noticing he had the flaring nose, olive skin, and soft brown eyes she was used to in the bayou country. Best of all, he had the kind demeanor of her Cajun neighbors. She wondered how much Maw-Maw had told him. By the compassionate way he was looking at her, she had an idea it was a lot.

"Pleased to meet you, Zachary," she said, looking right into his eyes, as she'd been taught in... where? Sunday school? School? Yes! They'd had a manners workshop one day.

Maw-Maw was almost squirming with delight. "What a well-mannered young lady," Zachary said. Cody nearly fainted with relief. She couldn't help it — she felt tainted by what she'd been for the last year and a half and knew she'd be viewed that way. She had to try harder to seem normal. She knew that. "Well-mannered young lady" was her new ideal. She wanted to look different, too.

"Zachary, join us," Maw-Maw said. "Let's have some breakfast while we plan our day."

Waiters brought everything you could want for breakfast, and Cody, having had no dinner last night — and little more than beans and rice for the last year and a half — ate every single thing, from the bacon to the pancakes.

"Baby, Zachary had an idea," Maw-Maw said. "He wants us all to spend some time together, and we thought... well, there'll be time enough to deal with... everything. Why don't we just play hooky today?"

Cody was speechless. If she could put off dealing with "everything" forever, she would. That wasn't going to happen, but a whole day? That was like a vacation in Paris.

"Sure," she said, trying to be cool, hoping she was somehow managing to cover up her eagerness. No, not even eagerness — her pure childlike joy.

"She's smiling," Zachary said. "I bet we might could talk her into it."

"What would you like to do?" Maw-Maw asked. "We

could kick back, maybe drive somewhere pretty, have a snowball at Miss Me-Me's, go see Molly and Kay at the bookstore... or we could get all ambitious and go to New Orleans."

Cody didn't much want to go back to New Orleans, but seeing people in Houma, people she knew, and having to tell her story — or more likely make one up — just wasn't something she could do today. "Could we get away?" She said. "I mean, out of town?"

"Hey," said Zachary. "You too old for the zoo?"

"The zoo!" The thought of animals and open space, maybe eating peanuts, suddenly seemed the most appealing thing in the world. And she'd never been to the zoo. "Could we do that?"

By the end of the day, she was pretty sure what Maw–Maw saw in Zachary, aside from the fact that he was a very handsome man. She was a little bit in love with him herself. When she really thought about it, he was the only grown man who'd ever been nice to her for more than a few minutes at a time. She'd never had a father and she couldn't remember her grandfather. There were teachers and neighbors, fathers of friends even, but all that was on the fly, really more politeness than actual interest in her. All day long, Zachary paid attention to her, made sure she was having fun, showed her things she might have missed, like the baby monkey in its mama's arms. He even asked if she was hungry or tired, like a father was supposed to, she thought. Or a grandfather.

I would love to have a grandfather. The thought was so foreign, seemed so unlikely, she hardly had the nerve to think it.

"Do you have grandchildren?" she asked.

He laughed like that was the funniest thing in the world.

"Do I have grandchirren! Cher! Ya might as well ax if I got fingers and toes. 'Cause that's how many I got — twenty! Twenty grandchirren and seven chirren."

"No wonder you're so good at it," she blurted, and felt herself blush.

He tousled her hair like she was a toddler. "How ya like the zoo?"

"Awesome!" Truthfully, it had probably been the best day of her life. She was so grateful to them for giving it to her before she had to start officially being a victim. And also a killer.

"Let's go get something to eat. Whatcha feel like?" She got to choose not only what she wanted (fried shrimp) but what kind of restaurant (seafood), and they went to a fancy place with white tablecloths. Her mother had never taken her to a place like that.

Both Maw-Maw and Zachary kissed her good night outside her room door, and Maw-Maw said, "Sleep tight, baby. We've got a big day tomorrow." Cody knew that meant they were going to have to go to the police. But she was too tired to be afraid right now. She could barely manage a shower.

Once again she slept deeply, but once more she woke up in the night, awakened by a dream — a nightmare involving a live green Buddha who was chasing her down a flight of stairs. But this time it was later — almost five a.m., and she couldn't get back to sleep. Lying there trying to forget the dream, forget the police, even forget Miguel, she felt a gnawing in her stomach. She was starving.

Not even bothering to change out of her cute new pajamas, she went exploring. Soft lighting kept the corridors from being a hazard for the arthritic, she supposed, and perhaps the staff moved around at night. She made her way down, wondering if they left the kitchen open.

She could get in, she found, and while the refrigerator seemed to be locked, some of the cupboards held pretzels and cookies, things evidently meant as snacks for the residents. Prowling a bit, she found bread for toast, and then peanut butter, a food she was heartily sick of — it was cheap and nourishing, perfect baby hooker food — but it would do fine for now.

Snack in hand, she sauntered into the library and sat down at the computer. Her first thought was to figure out where to get a phone and then how to get there, but suddenly she realized she might be able to figure out who she'd killed. She thought she knew, but when she really thought about it, it had to be impossible — the guy she thought it was was famous. Important. Had she really killed someone like that?

Searching for "New Orleans news", she ended up at a news site that gave her a "crime" option. She clicked on it. Yes! There it was: "Man Found Dead on Magazine Street." But there was something strange here. It said he died of asphyxiation, probably as the result of a chokehold. But she'd beaten him to death — hadn't she? Was there any way she could have smothered him? She looked carefully at his name — Benjamin Solo. Wait! Was that Benny? She didn't know his last name, but what were the chances he and the whale had the same name? Something was seriously wrong here.

If Benny was dead, she had worse problems than the cops. Miguel was coming after her.

Cody tried to work out what had happened. Benny definitely wasn't the man she'd beaten with the Buddha. So... how had his body replaced the other guy's? True, she didn't know for a fact the whale was dead, but... hey, if he wasn't, then she hadn't killed anybody. That had to be good.

Could the whale have killed Benny? But why would he? And how? She could have sworn she'd beaten the hell out of him, but maybe she wasn't as strong as she thought. He was a really big guy.

Sweat pouring off her, she tried to think. Her mom had sold her to a local low-life she knew only as Calvin, who had taken her immediately to Miguel. Just kind of a whore-broker, she thought — and now that she was back in Bible-land, she wondered: whoremonger? Was that what a whore-monger was? Stop, she told herself. Focus. She'd been pretty much comatose with shock, but she could remember Miguel and Calvin laughing and joking together, just because it was such a contrast with her own misery. They were definitely friends.

Miguel had to know where Calvin was from, but he wouldn't even have to come after him, he could just ask him who Cody's mom was. He'd expect Cody to go back home, probably, run to her family. Anybody would. And once he knew her mom's name, Miguel could find Maw-Maw almost as easily as Cody had. Come to think of it, Calvin knew all about Maw-Maw, might even know where she'd moved to.

Cody's stomach turned over. Had she put her grand-mother in danger? No question she was in danger, and she didn't want Maw-Maw caught in the crossfire. But she could fix this. She could see several ways. The first was the police, as planned, but that might not be fast enough. Even if they picked up Miguel just on her say-so, they were going to grill her for a few hours first. Who knew what else they were going to do? Maybe they'd hold her overnight, or send her back to New Orleans, or make her go to a hospital to get checked out for rape and STDs.

But wait! The police could help. If Miguel was still in town, she could see a way to speed up that process. And if he wasn't, then she could go to them with Maw-Maw like they'd planned. Just tomorrow instead of today. The Houston cops would get him, and sometime down the line, she'd testify against him, and they'd lock him up and throw away the key.

But she had to have a phone! There was a little office on this floor, maybe there was one there.

But of course it was locked.

She knew she could get a phone at Wal-Mart, one of those pre-paid ones like Miguel always had, but could she get to Wal-Mart? She found a map online that indicated she couldn't walk there. But she could walk to the Greyhound Bus Station. She went upstairs to get dressed, all the while thinking, making and remaking her plan, working out contingencies.

To leave a note or not? She had to. There was just no way she could disappoint Maw-Maw and Zachary any more than she had to. So she said not to worry and she'd be back by evening. She addressed it to Maw-Maw, left it in the room, and slipped out of the building after sunrise.

It was a beautiful morning, a little cool, but by most standards downright tropical for January. Evidently there hadn't been a freeze so far. Instead of brown and bent, the plants in the yards and parkways looked fresh and green, some even studded with pansies or those little spiky flowers that looked like stars — no one had ever told her what they were called. The air felt fresh too — it could get so hot in Texas. The truth was, she was enjoying herself. It was great to be free and on a mission — even kind of a grim mission.

Spotting a group of people waiting at a bus stop, she tapped the one who looked the most likely to her, a boy about her age, black and self-important, eyes darting every-where to see who was noting his young, handsome, desirable self. "Hey," she said.

"Hey." He answered in such a low voice she could barely hear, like he was surprised to be spoken to. Well, she had more surprises.

"How'd you like to make twenty bucks?"

"Huh?"

"All you have to do is lend me your phone for a minute."

Slowly, without speaking, he handed it over, like he thought she was going back on the offer. She popped a twenty-dollar bill into his hand. "How do I call information?"

"You stupid or something?"

"No, I forgot how. I've been in jail. Quick," she snapped. "Before the bus comes."

His eyes widened, but he shrugged and told her.

"Bayou Motel in New Orleans," she said. One more call and she had what she needed: Miguel was still there.

Okay, then. Plan B it was. She gave the kid back his phone and strode purposefully to the Greyhound Bus Station. But she wasn't fast enough — she missed the only morning bus. That wasn't the end of the world — it just meant she was going to have to take a bus to somewhere else and transfer. She wouldn't get to New Orleans till afternoon, but what else did she have to do?

Well, eat breakfast, so she did that. Next stop: one of her old, most dreaded haunts. Oddly, she wasn't scared a bit. She felt surprisingly in control.

The first part of her plan called for finally buying a cell phone and she'd figured out online there was a Walmart right in the center of the city. She got a taxi at the bus station, took it there, and was surprised when the driver asked if she wanted him to wait. She hadn't known they could do that, but she had enough money, so why not?

There was sure a wide choice of burner phones. In the end, she'd settled on one that could text and had a camera, but no Internet access. She hoped she wouldn't regret going the cheap route.

Her plan was simple but foolproof, she was pretty sure. Unless of course Miguel or Lloyd saw her and snatched her again. But she was feeling a lot more confident the last two days. She could handle this. She even had a plan in case she ran into them — scream like a banshee.

"The Bayou Motel," she told the driver, feeling bold and ready. Her game plan was simply this — call Miguel's room to make sure he was in there, then call the police from some safe spot and say he'd kidnapped her. They'd have to come, wouldn't they? They'd see she had no I.D., and they'd drag her in, but here was the beauty part — they'd drag Miguel in too. Then she could call Maw-Maw and Zachary and they could all sort it out with Miguel safely in jail. They might send her to juvie, or do heaven knew what else with her, but she'd at least keep Miguel from coming after her and maybe hurting Maw-Maw. Simple, she thought, but perfect. She couldn't see a flaw in it.

But as they got close, it became apparent something was happening. The place was overrun with police cars, red lights reflecting on the ugly stucco of the building. That was going to wreck everything! Nobody was going to care about her with a serious crime happening there.

They couldn't get into the parking lot, not at all what she had in mind. She wondered if it was safe to get out and see what she could find out. And then she saw it wasn't. Lloyd was watching from a distance, smoking a cigarette with his shirt off. Pig, she thought.

The driver said, "Looks like something's going on. Want me to wait for you again?"

"Hey, can we just hang here a few minutes?"

"Whatever floats your boat." She hated that expression.

She watched Lloyd smoke his cigarette and go back into his room, which was next to Miguel's, the one where Cody had been kept along with two other girls. The door to Miguel's room opened and a tall woman came out, wearing black pants and a dark green blazer, a crown of curls falling to her collar. Behind her was a man in a suit, about the same height as the woman, very slender, and from what Cody could see, quite handsome.

They joined a knot of cops, and it dawned on her that they were also cops and that meant whatever had happened involved Miguel. She saw the woman nod and then in response, a team wheeled a gurney into the room.

The cabbie stared at her, obviously getting impatient, finally shrugged, and made a phone call in a language she didn't recognize. Cody kept her eyes glued to the room until long after he'd finished the call — in fact, till they wheeled the body out. The body, she imagined, that could only be Miguel. One of the girls could have died, but why wouldn't the girls be back in Houston by now?

She had butterflies like she was about to go onstage or something. Could this really be happening? It could mean she was finally and definitely free, never going back, no chance. Couldn't it? She felt a catch in the back of her throat.

But the weird thing was, she didn't see how Miguel could have died — he wasn't sick; and the only drug she'd ever seen him do was pot. So... if not overdose or illness, then what? Did she dare let herself think about that?

Because that road led to the whale. And if the whale had killed Miguel...

"Lady, you going in or what?" the cabbie asked.

"I think I changed my mind. Why don't you drop me in the French Quarter? Somewhere near Jackson Square." It was the only location she knew.

She needed to think this through, and also she needed to see Terry. What she'd done to her was increasingly on her mind. Someone who'd steal from her only friend just wasn't who Cody was. She'd done it in a panic, in a different reality — one in which her mother was alive and Maw-Maw might not be, and she didn't know what would happen to her. She might have to live on the street. She felt more secure now, as if she had a home of sorts — at least she knew someone loved her and knew her story, would try to find her, even go to the police if she disappeared again. That made things look a lot different, and she was more and more ashamed of what she'd done.

She had to return the money. Just had to before she could go back to Houma and face Maw-Maw. Maybe the ID too — although that was going to hurt. She used her new phone to call her grandmother and leave a message, saying not to worry, she'd be home tomorrow.

Then she walked. Up and down the beautiful streets, just taking them in. And thinking. She'd always found walking helped her think. Like taking a shower.

She had an idea about where she could stay — Elliott and Mikey, the guys who'd helped her find Terry, had said there was a place she could go to, where they wouldn't turn her in. Covenant House. She'd made a pretty careful mental note about that.

But how to get to Terry? Going to her house was out of the question. She was too ashamed. She could go to Daddy's

Girls and leave the money in an envelope, but two problems with that— she didn't trust anyone there to deliver it. And she didn't have an envelope.

Well, she could get an envelope, but still... who could she trust? Pretty soon, a face came to her, a seriously cranky one. "Yes!" She pumped her arm and yelled, way too loud. She'd somehow made her way to a street with a lot of clubs, like Bourbon Street but smaller, and there were a lot of people about. Most didn't even seem to notice. But a few stared. And a guy in a car screeched to a stop and got out. "Hey!" he yelled. She stared, but only for a second. That was enough before she took off running. It was the whale. Same dark skin. Same shaved head. Same intimidating persona and tall heavy build.

She pounded down the sidewalk, his heavy footsteps thumping behind her. But there was a lot of other noise too — honking and yelling. Stuff like, "Move your fucking car, dickhead!" She wondered if she should just duck in someplace before she ran out of businesses. It looked like the small strip stopped at the end of the block. Surely he wouldn't kill her in front of other people.

And then the thumping stopped. She didn't stop to look behind her, just kept flying. And finally she nearly fell through the doors of a restaurant, the last one, it looked like, before the area became residential.

"Are you okay?" the hostess said. She was so well-dressed she made Cody feel shabby, even in her pain. And she was in pain, her chest spasming from all that unaccustomed running. Miguel hadn't exactly bought his captives gym memberships. She bent over, hands on her knees, trying to catch her breath.

"Let me get you some water," the woman said.

"No!" Cody blurted, and was embarrassed that it came

out as a yell. And that she had grabbed the woman. "Don't leave me," she said in a lower voice. "He's chasing me."

The woman's brows went up. Her eyes, already painted wide open, grew rounder still. She stepped to the door to look. "That big guy?" She said. "He's getting in his car. Kinda looks like... naaah, it couldn't be. You okay?" she said again.

Cody stood up, breath still coming in spurts.

"What happened?" the hostess said. "I'm going to get that water."

But she didn't have to leave. The bartender, having silently watched the whole scene, handed her a glass. She passed it to Cody, who sipped gratefully. "Should we call the cops?" the bartender asked.

Cody considered. Really considered. But if they called the cops, she was going to have to tell them enough of the story that they'd take her to a police station and she'd have to ride in the back of the car. Living among criminals, committing every single day what Miguel told her were her own crimes, had conditioned her to fear that more than grizzlies, sharks, or space aliens.

She didn't think she could do it. And if she did do it, her vow to reimburse Terry would never be kept. She wondered if the whale was out there waiting for her.

"No thanks," she said, "but could you call me a cab?"

The face she'd seen when she shouted, inadvertently attracting the whale's attention, the seriously cranky face, was the one on Solomon Clark, the corner store guy who'd made his nephew drive her to Houma. She was pretty sure she could trust him to give Terry the money — especially if she paid him to do it. Solomon struck her as a dude who didn't give away much, but he wouldn't steal either. Otherwise, he'd have had his nephew rob her.

She had in mind doing the waiting thing again —

having the taxi wait while she struck a deal with Solomon — but she wanted to first make sure the whale wasn't still around. He had a blue car, she thought. She had the driver do a wild goose chase kind of drive for twenty minutes or so till she was sure there were no blue cars following.

When they got to the store, Lamar was at the counter, not his uncle. "Hey, Lamar," she said.

"Hey," Lamar answered, casting a sullen glance at the floor, not giving the slightest hint he had a clue who she was.

"Solomon around?"

"Nope." Now he met her eyes. "It's me or nobody." The snotty way he sounded said it all — he remembered her perfectly well and this time he didn't have to be nice. Well, Lamar she didn't trust. If she gave him the hundred bucks, plus ten for delivery, he'd end up a hundred and ten dollars richer.

"You got an envelope?" she asked.

"You mean for free?"

"I'll buy one."

"You gotta buy a box."

So she bought a box, plus a ballpoint pen.

Then she got in the cab, wrote Terry a note on one envelope, then stuck it and the money in another, still hesitating about the Lucy Valdez license. Finally she stuck that in too. In for a penny, in for a pound, her mama used to say. Probably got it from Maw-Maw.

She had a new plan: She'd have the driver wait while she stuck the envelope in the mailbox and ran like hell back to the cab. If Terry saw her, no problem, she could still run like hell.

She had her entire arm in the mailbox when Terry

grabbed her. Cody hadn't even heard the door open. "Get in here, you little shit!"

She nearly tore Cody's arm off, dragging her inside and closing the door. "Winston! Look who's back. Little Miss No Good Deed Goes Unpunished."

"Terry, I feel terrible. I came here to..."

Terry turned to face her, features practically purple, a mask of fury. She crouched like a cat. "I put you up and you steal my money? What kinda shit is that?"

"I'm so sorry, I came back to..." Cody rubbed her sore arm, backing away. Terry looked as if she might jump her. But she didn't see Winston coming at her from behind. He shoved her to the floor before she even knew he was there, and climbed on top of her, closing his fist. She shut her eyes, turning her head so he wouldn't smash her front teeth.

"Get off her! Jesus, Winston, you can't do that!" Terry yelled, but he didn't move.

Instead he froze. They could all hear footsteps.

And then someone pounded on the door, loud, hard and authoritatively, like the police. Cody wondered briefly if her driver'd called them, but he probably hadn't had time.

Winston jumped to a squat and stood in two athletic motions. Then he started kicking her, hard. He'd landed two good blows before Terry pulled him off.

"Who brought you here, bitch? What kinda shit's about to come in our door? You brought the po-lice?"

"I think it's just my... boy friend," she said impulsively, thinking that sounded more dangerous than "driver". She sat up and leaned on the coffee table, getting her breath. On it was a card with an address written on it. The card was for a gym, but the address had been added in pencil. She might not have even noticed, except that it was underlined twice, emphatically. As it was, she barely registered it, only realized it rang a distant bell, but nothing she could place.

When she could breathe properly, she hoisted herself and ran to the door, half-expecting to be grabbed and hit or kicked again. But she made it and left without even closing the door. Her driver was already halfway back to the cab.

When she caught up, she thanked him for coming after her.

"You kidding?" he said. "You didn't pay the fare."

She got in the car. "Wait a minute!" she said.

"I did something wrong? You don't pay, what you think? I'm not gonna come after ya?"

"Oh, sorry. I wasn't talking to you."

"Huh?"

"I mean I just thought of something. Hey, can you do me a favor? Can you look up an address for me? My phone's, like, just a flip." She felt weirdly apologetic about not having a smart phone.

"Sure, I could do that." She gave him the address she'd just seen on the card.

12

———

First Miguel's death and Lloyd's arrest, then, barely a day later, during her nice January "barbecue," Abasolo's phone call. Sometimes it seemed like one step backward for every step forward. The Whale was on the move again.

Skip couldn't believe what she was looking at. Or rather she didn't want to. She didn't even want to be a cop today. She wanted to walk time back and arrange to be out of the country so she wouldn't have to see this. Because it was ugly and terrifying and heralded so many more bad things she felt her throat close and nausea roil her stomach.

There were two bodies in the little house, but that wasn't what was causing the waves of fear and horror that were currently washing over her. It was on a bedroom wall:

"Blackass bitch spicaninny snigger mexcrement batman diaperhead BMO."

"The whale, for sure," Abasolo said. "We're fucked."

"Yeah. It's starting."

It was obvious to both of them: the wannabe serial killer who'd first attacked the dog and then the pink-haired girl —

and probably killed Benjamin Solo — had now achieved his goal. He'd embarked on a killing spree that wasn't going to stop until they got him.

Skip's stomach turned over again, thinking how many people could be in danger, how much panic could ensue — and how much responsibility she had.

"What do you bet it's like before?" Abasolo said. "The lady in the bed —" he gestured with his head "—will be a hooker and the gentleman out there will turn out to be her pimp, who rented this place through Airbnb?"

"Not taking that bet," she said, barely able to get the words out. "Anyway, we already know it's Airbnb." She'd worked a serial case once before. It sucked.

Evidently seeing her distress, Abasolo kept talking. "He really did a number on her."

Her skin was flayed and clearly had bled in some places. Her body looked misshapen around the ribcage, like a rubber doll someone had squeezed and broken. Broken. That was how she looked.

She was small and this time undeniably African-American — possibly more his ideal victim than the pink-haired girl. The man on the floor in the living room looked as if he could have been mideastern — if so, representing another of this creep's prejudices. If you called it a prejudice when someone was killing members of minority groups he didn't like. And if that was what was happening here. Once again Skip wondered, as she had that day in the yoga studio — were these hate crimes? Surely that couldn't be the whole story! Hate killers could be mass murderers, but serial killers had a special psychology — and one much different from the perpetrators of hate crimes. Or so she'd always thought.

Hearing steps in the hall, she turned to see who was

coming. "Hey, y'all," said Permelia Read. "This is a cute place."

It was. It was one of the oh-so-contemporary restorations happening all over town right now, particularly in the Second District — a double shotgun that had been gutted and turned into a welcoming single with an open floor plan and plenty of Cararra marble in the kitchen.

And then Read saw the writing. "Oh, shit. Him again. Well, that explains that furious woman outside. Airbnb again, huh? She must be the owner."

"Yeah. This lady wasn't as lucky as the last one. And neither was her friend in the living room."

"Any I.D.'s for these guys?"

"No. It's like last time. He must have taken them."

Abasolo had wandered off. "Hey, guys," he called. "Check this out. There's a note in the kitchen to 'Airbnb tenants,' with a name and phone number."

Read just shrugged and got to work in the bedroom.

Skip joined Abasolo. The note was signed by an Emily Martinez. The district cops who'd called homicide had told them the owner discovered the bodies, but on the way in they'd ignored the furious woman who'd impressed Read. Now that Skip thought about it, fury seemed an odd reaction to finding two bodies in your house. "Let's go talk to her," she said.

Emily Martinez was dressed in jeans, flip-flops, and a faded-out man's Henley T-shirt. Her hair was in a ponytail and she wore no make-up. She was screeching like a bird on her cellphone, forehead squinched up like she was in pain. At her feet was a small duffel.

Seeing Skip and Abasolo, she quickly ended her phone call and strode over to them. "This is my house," she said. "What the hell is going on here?"

Skip resisted the temptation to catch Abasolo's eye. "You're the owner?"

"I just told you I am."

"You're Emily Martinez?" Abasolo said. He was messing with her. A bit unprofessional, but she had it coming.

"Goddammit, yes. Whathehell is happening in there?" She was practically jumping up and down, as if being attacked by fire ants.

Abasolo spoke slowly and infuriatingly. "I'm Lieutenant Adam Abasolo."

Skip followed his lead, slowing things down just because. "Sergeant Skip Langdon. Do you live here alone?"

"Sergeant, why the hell are two people dead in my house?"

"We hear you called in a double murder."

"I found them when I got here. I rented the place out to an Airbnb tenant who checked out at noon."

"He did? You talked to him or her after they checked out?"

"Him. Of course not. But they always leave on time. Who are these people and how did they get in?"

She sneaked a glance at Abasolo; she couldn't help it. Very carefully, she said, "Is there any possibility they're your Airbnb tenants? Did you actually see the tenants?"

For the first time, she looked uncomfortable. "No, Mr. Jones asked me to leave the key in the mailbox. In an envelope."

Abasolo said, "Jones."

"Kenneth Jones."

"How did you communicate with him?"

"It's done by email. Haven't you ever done it?"

"Of course not," Skip said, "It's illegal."

"It is not! Everybody does it."

"Actually, I think you can get a license for it now. But up till this month it's been illegal."

She looked at Skip the way you look at a person who claims to have been abducted by aliens.

Abasolo picked up the thread. "So you never saw or spoke with the tenant?"

"You think it's *those* people?" Emily sounded furious. "Are you kidding me? This is an extremely high-end rental."

"Are you saying," Skip asked, "that that poor woman in there isn't good enough to die in your house? Is that what you're saying?"

"Of course that's not what I'm..." she stopped in mid-sentence. "You know what? I'm going to report you. You can't talk to me like that."

Skip thought, *It's deja vu all over again*. Very seldom did anyone threaten to report her, but Dustin De Blanc had. What was it about this case?

Fortunately she had Abasolo to turn on his famous charm. In a few minutes they'd learned that Emily was a nurse but liked to make a little money renting out her house, so she stayed at her mom's on those occasions, and without that extra money, she'd probably have to give up her planned trip to Las Vegas with two high school friends, so really she needed to do it whether it was legal or not, and she was just sure the dead people inside couldn't possibly be her tenants, who must have departed early, leaving the key in the mailbox where anyone could get it.

"Stranger things have happened," Abasolo said, managing not to roll his eyes, indeed to look perfectly sincere. Skip had to admire him.

But Emily wasn't done. "That man in there?" she said. "I'm pretty sure he's Hispanic. America should be for Americans or we wouldn't have these kinds of problems."

Skip spoke up again. Every partnership needed a bad cop. "Mrs. Martinez," she asked innocently, "pardon me, but aren't you Hispanic yourself?"

"Why would you think that? I'm as American as you are."

"Your name?"

"That's my ex's name. And he's as American as football!"

"So... you have something against people who aren't American?"

"Not in their own countries I don't."

Abasolo caught her eye, tilted one brow ever so slightly. Skip gave him the go-ahead. "I want to show you something. I'll be right back."

In the interim Skip learned what Emily thought of political correctness and certain people trying to take advantage of the ones who worked for a living, and then Abasolo produced the photo he'd just taken. "Did you write this?" he asked.

"What is that?"

"That's a picture of your guest room wall."

"No, it's not. I was in there. I didn't see that." She took the phone and held it closer. "'Spicaninny'? Does that mean what I think it means? Whathehell is that? That's not on my wall."

Skip sighed. Emily couldn't be the whale — could she? She thought back to what she knew of serial killers. The organized ones didn't even kill in their own neighborhoods, much less their own homes. To do something that crazy, Emily would have to be decompensating at a pretty rapid rate.

Emily laughed. "'Mexcrement'? That's pretty good." But then she seemed to realize what was happening. "Hey, what are you guys saying? Just 'cause I don't like trashy people I'd kill 'em?"

"It looks like somebody did," Skip said.

Emily really gave her pause. Given the right environment, who knew what direction a twisted mind might take?

She shook off the thought. There had to be more to it. There always was. But the last few months there'd been so many hate crimes...

WHEN IT STARTED to get dark, Cody went to Covenant House, wondering if they served dinner there.

Tanya, the young woman at the desk, was so nice you'd have thought Cody was an honored guest. Way friendlier than Cody would have expected. She almost acted as if she knew Cody. "Heeeeeeey. What can I do for you? Come on in and get comfortable. Sure we can help you."

She took her to a smaller room to talk and asked a few friendly questions about what had brought Cody there. All was fine until she said, "Let me get you a counselor." She texted as she spoke.

"I don't want a counselor, I just need..."

"Oh, don't worry, everybody has to talk to Melody, you know? I mean, if people have to have medication, we need to know about it. And we have to get their personal info— like names and next of kin, you know? It's like when you check into a hotel."

Cody had every idea it was nothing like that, and she was somewhat bothered that Tanya didn't leave to summon Melody, but texted instead. What was up with that? Cody was free now, right? So why couldn't she be left alone?

And then Melody breezed in, right hand stuck out to

shake. She was a long-haired blonde, wearing dangly bead earrings and beat-up jeans, with an air of perfect confidence — and something else. Something Cody couldn't put her finger on — it seemed like a compassion that spilled over into... what? A kind of overeagerness, she thought. Maybe Melody seemed a little too eager to help? Like Tanya. Cody liked her immediately. But for some reason, she was also intimidated.

"Hi, I heard you were here. I'm Melody." Tanya slipped quietly out and Melody took her chair.

Sitting directly across from her, Cody could see she had a beautiful, open face with nothing but kindness showing on it. Still... there was something. Cody just didn't trust her.

Melody waited a moment. Finally she said, "Can I ask your name?"

Cody hadn't thought this out. She hadn't thought about having to give out information to stay here. And, weirdly, Tanya hadn't asked. She wondered why.

Well, no problem coming up with a name. There were a dozen nicknames for Cordelia, and Cody knew them all. CoCo, Cordy, Cora, Corey, Dee, Dee-Dee, Delia... Delia was way too old-fashioned, but if you shortened it, there were two good ones. Should she be Dia or Lia?

"Dia," she said, "Dia Boudreaux." About the most common last name in Louisiana. "You're the counselor?"

Melody looked momentarily taken aback, but so briefly you could almost swear it hadn't happened. "I'm the director," she said.

"Tanya said counselor."

Melody's smile only grew broader. "She's a new volunteer. I think she didn't know what to say — I don't usually meet with the guests."

Cody's antennae went up. "Why me?" She struggled to keep it casual.

"Well, first of all, you should know that we have a policy of not calling your parents, not calling... anyone..."

"Like the police? Or ICE?"

Melody looked horrified. "We'd never call ICE. I'd have to be dead first." She put her elbows on the table and rested her chin on her palms, which brought her face down even closer to Melody's, and should have made her less intimidating. But Cody's neck was prickling. "And not the police. You can stay as long as you like and you can leave at any time. We're here to help kids, not turn them over to the system. But... look, let me just say it: we can help if you're in danger. And... I think you might be, am I right?"

Cody felt two big tears start up and spill over onto her cheeks. She nodded.

Melody answered carefully, almost one word at a time, speaking so low Cody almost couldn't hear her, as if afraid she might spook like a horse. "We know. The police know. You got away from a murderer, didn't you, baby? And probably a pimp. Actually, a whole gang of pimps — Lloyd, Benny, and Miguel — and they're never going to hurt you again." She abandoned her walking-on-eggs persona, smiled like she really meant it, and said in a normal tone, "That took guts!"

The dam Cody had built inside herself shattered as if bombed. Her whole body shook with sobs, mucous poured from her nose, half her body liquid flowed out of her eyes. And she howled. The sobs were one thing, some sort of involuntary body spasm that wouldn't stop, but the howling was all hers. She had cried with Maw-Maw, but even then she hadn't been able to tell the whole story. It was dammed up inside her, wedged in there like a fortune in a vault, the only thing between herself and her hard-won freedom. Once she thought it was safe to let it out, her anguish — all the pain and loneliness and loss of the last two years, her fear, all the tension of being on the edge of hysteria as she fought her way out of that terrifying apartment with the writing on the wall, all the terror that the traffickers would come after Maw-Maw — escaped out her throat as she howled like an animal.

Melody held her for most of that time, as soon as she could maneuver herself around the table between them, and she never once shushed her or patted her like she should just shut up, just provided a warm human to hold onto. And finally the howling stopped and the wracking sobs turned into great huge gasps aimed at getting some air back in her body, and the world around her came into focus. "Oh," she said, as if she'd spilled something. "I've been screaming. I'm so sorry."

Melody said, "Baby, you scream all you want. That's what we're here for."

"I must have scared people."

"No. Everybody who comes here has something chasing them — even if it's their crime partner or their stepfather. Everybody in here knows what you're feeling."

Cody wasn't so sure of that.

13

From a side table, Melody got her some water from a sleek carafe with a spigot, the kind of dispenser Maw-Maw used to serve lemonade from, and asked if she was hungry. Cody hesitated, sure she couldn't possibly be hungry, and suddenly, once the thought was introduced, felt her insides yawn like a cave. She was starving.

"Yes," she said. "I think I am."

Melody laughed at that and went to ask Tanya to bring them both some food. While they ate their egg salad sandwiches and crunched potato chips, Melody tried some light probing — could she call someone for Cody? Where was Cody from? – but Cody was having none of it. She wanted to tell it — all of it. The howls were only the beginning. But she couldn't do that till she knew a few things herself.

"How do you know about the pimps?" she asked abruptly.

"I have a friend. Don't freak out — she's a really good friend and you absolutely don't have to meet her until you're ready — but she's a cop. She knew a girl had to be there because of the evidence at the crime scene." While Cody was trying to process that, she explained, "Where they found Benjamin Solo. The place on Magazine St."

Cody shuddered. "Weird place. It only had furniture in one room."

Melody laughed. "It's a yoga studio, that's why."

"Oh. Right." The pieces clicked into place, and Cody even smiled. "Sure. Well, that's not creepy, then, but the wall…"

"Yes, the writing. Skip told me."

"Skip?"

"My friend. You want to see a picture of her?" Melody fished a phone from her jeans pocket and flipped to a picture of a happy-looking woman, a good-sized one with lots of curly hair, kissing a beautiful long-eared dog, like a cocker spaniel but prettier.

She registered somewhere in the back of her mind that this was one of the cops she'd seen at the Buy-Me, but her attention went elsewhere.

"Awwww— how adorable!"

"Rambla, you mean? That's Skip and Steve's dog. She's a star! But Skip's pretty adorable too. She saved my life when I was about your age. Literally." She was nodding, as if answering an unanswered question. "I've known her that long. If there's one person in the world you can trust, it's Skip Langdon."

Cody knew what she was trying to do, but she went ahead and let it work on her. There was something undeniably appealing about a cop with a cute dog. And a husband or boy friend. But she wasn't going to let herself be distracted. "What was the evidence? You know — that led to me?"

"The hair, mostly. They found some in the yoga studio. It's pretty distinctive. That's how Tracy knew you when you came in. Skip asked us to look out for a girl with pink and brown curly hair."

That was why they'd seemed overeager, Cody realized. Because they were all looking for her.

At the mention of her hair, she teared up again. She wanted normal hair so bad! "Miguel had women come in and do slutty stuff to our hair. I don't even know if they were real hairdressers. Could have been his mom and aunt for all I know. I hate this pink thing, don't you?"

"Not so much right now — it's the main way we found you."

"So Benny was the only dead guy?"

"At the yoga studio, yes. Miguel's dead too, but he died at a fleabag motel."

"The Bayou. That's where they kept us when we were in town."

"That's it. Could have been a suicide. He died of a heroin overdose."

"No way! He was too mean for that. It was either an accident or..."

"Well, they don't think it was that. The room was tossed, like someone was looking for something."

"What I don't get is, how did Benny die?"

Melody hesitated. She chewed on her lip before she answered. "I think maybe you and Skip should talk about that."

Slowly it dawned on Cody what she meant. "Wait! The cops think I killed him?"

"I didn't say that."

"I didn't kill Benny. I killed the other guy."

As soon as Skip saw the girl, she wanted nothing so much as to give her a hug and say everything would be okay. She was so slight, so bedraggled, so fearful — so much the epitome of a tired child, one who'd been traveling a long, long time. She knew it was going to take a lot more than a hug to make everything okay for this kid — maybe nothing ever would. But she doubted that. Despite clearly having been banged around by life, she looked far from defeated. Her eyes shone with the alertness of a newly-minted kitten and her jaw had a real determination going on — a hard set you don't often see in someone so young — that said whatever had to be done, she'd do it.

Skip didn't doubt that for a moment. She'd spent quite a bit of time trying to figure out what the kid had done. Skip knew it wasn't going to be easy for her to spill her guts to a couple of cops, but she had arranged a small surprise she hoped would make it easier.

"Dia Boudreaux," Melody said, "meet my friend Skip." No "sergeant" involved, Skip noticed. Nice move.

"And this handsome gentleman is Adam Abasolo," she said, taking Melody's cue and leaving out his rank.

A.A. really had a friendly smile — he was so charming partly because he was so sincere, and he gave the kid full wattage. Plus a firm handshake. "Dia, it's a pleasure."

Skip fought the urge to hug — at this point with a juvenile anything could be considered assault — and also settled for a handshake, but she let her words be as emotional as she felt. "Girl, you don't know how worried we've been about you!"

The kid's eyes filled, and Skip could have kicked herself. She tried to make it better. "You're going to be ok now. No one can hurt you any more."

The girl gave a little smile.

"Melody, she reminds me of you at her age."

Melody laughed. "I know. Me too."

"Is that a compliment?" the kid asked.

Skip said, "Big-time."

"Oh, yeah?" said Melody. "Tell us more."

"You weren't afraid of anything."

"Oh, yes, I was."

"Me too," the kid whispered. "Lots of stuff."

Skip caught a brief glimpse of A.A.'s face before he turned away to hide it. She could see he was thinking of the time the kid had spent in slavery. Quickly, she pushed the thought out of her own head. Last thing she needed was the entire Homicide Division dissolving on the floor.

And just in time the cavalry arrived, in the form of Skip's surprise. She heard a distinctive scrambling, toenails on bare floor, and barely glimpsed a waving white tail before she was ambushed by Rambla, now barking loudly for attention. As one, the entire department rose, many of them with smiles on their hard-cop faces.

"Awww, a therapy dog," LePage said. "Is that for me?" He stared down at Rambla and talked to her. "Come on, poochie, over here. I'm having a pretty traumatic day."

Skip tried to look embarrassed. "Ummm... doggy day care got out early today. Sorry, guys, looks like I'm up." She waved to Steve, who'd appeared in the doorway. He threw her the leash. "Mission accomplished," he mouthed, and disappeared.

"Dia," Skip said, "this is Rambla."

"I know," she said. "I saw her picture." She reached down for the dog's neck, looking hungry, like she wanted a lot more.

"I've got an idea," Skip said. "Let's find an interview room. Rambla, heel."

When the door was closed and all four were inside —
five counting Rambla — Skip dropped to the floor and
cuddled her dog. "Come on," she said to the kid. "It's okay.
No one can see us in here."

The kid dropped down and Rambla gave her a big
welcoming kiss on the nose, almost knocking her over.
Squeals ensued — high-pitched, delighted girlish ones, the
sort that ought to come out of a teen-ager. Rambla cuddled
delightedly, then began howling gently like she did when
greeting somebody she hadn't seen for a while. When Skip
judged girl and dog had had a long enough necking session,
she said, "We can talk down here if you like — do you want
to hold Rambla?"

"Sure, I wouldn't mind," the kid said, all nonchalant like
it was nothing, but Skip noticed one of her hands went
protectively around the little canine body and the other
moved rhythmically from neck to tail, never seeming to tire.

She set up her microphone on the floor and said, "Can
you state your full name and address?"

Whereupon the kid got teary again. Who knew that was
a hard question?

"I think... I might be homeless," she stammered. "My
mom passed away. You know I escaped from somewhere,
right? Melody told you?"

"Yes, we know the background. I'm sorry to hear about
your mom. Let's try it this way: we understand from Melody
that you were trafficked to Houston by a man named Miguel
Bustamente, who forced you into prostitution for almost
two years. Is that true?"

She wasn't supposed to do that. She was supposed to get
the kid to tell her. But this wasn't about that case, and she
just didn't have the heart to make her say it.

Even hearing it seemed to cause a panic that made her

hold Rambla so tight she squeaked. Skip looked down and could see the kid blinking for a while. Finally, she whispered, "Yes."

"Okay, then, let's just start in January. Why were you in New Orleans?"

The kid took a deep breath and sat up straight, as if she were telling herself, "let's do this thing!"

She spoke haltingly, sometimes several seconds passing between words. "Miguel and a man named Lloyd brought me and some other girls to the Sugar Bowl. They turned me over to a man named Benny for a... ummm... a trick..." She looked up at that, to see how the word was received, and Skip saw that she was blushing... "but this wasn't the usual set-up. This was in a rented apartment and I had to wear something special and be posed a certain way..."

"Can you tell about that?" Skip asked.

Slowly, very slowly, the story came out — how the customer had attacked her, how she'd beaten him with the green Buddha and escaped out the back, how she'd left the gym bag at The Palace Café and then gone on to find a friend to stay with. And then, suddenly, she seemed to run out of steam, to diminish in size like a punctured balloon.

"I'll get some water," Abasolo said.

The kid stood up. "Can I go to the bathroom?"

Melody said, "Sure. I'll take you."

While everyone was gone, Skip wondered how she was going to keep the kid out of the dreaded System — whether the timing was right to ask her about relatives so she didn't have to go into foster care.

Rambla perked up as steps approached, moving fast. And then Melody exploded into the room, the girl right behind her, neither looking good, the kid pale as a piece of paper. "What happened?"

"Dia's sick. I've got to take her back."

Skip gave her a quizzical look.

"She started throwing up as soon as we got there. Stress, I guess."

"Okay, then, go! Dia, you rock, you know that? Go lie down and feel better." She turned to Melody. "Talk later?"

"Tomorrow at the latest."

But it wasn't twenty minutes before she was on the phone. "Dia's gone."

"Whathehell?"

"We were at a stoplight and she jumped out of the car and started running. I drove around trying to find her, but she wanted to disappear and... I guess she did."

Skip was dumbfounded. "What happened there?"

"I guess... maybe she wanted to tell her story, but didn't want to risk you calling Child Protective Services."

"You think she's sophisticated enough to know that could even happen?"

"Are you kidding? She's been living with no one but teen-age hookers and criminals. Stories get told."

"I thought she really liked Rambla," Skip lamented.

LATER, walking Rambla with Steve, she was still puzzling over it. "She did great. She never let go of Rambla and told the whole damn story without squeezing her to death. Then, out of the clear blue, she fakes being sick and runs away. What happened there?"

"Something spooked her?" Steve suggested.

Skip thought back to the conversation. "I sure can't think of anything. There was a time when she seemed to kind of run out of gas, but nobody had said anything to her — it was just Dia doing the talking. Although Melody thought maybe she was worried about falling into the system." Something disturbing caught her eye. "Hey! Whatehell is that?"

She pointed to a fence with graffiti that said, "STAMP OUT POLITICAL CORRECTNESS! KILL A LIBERAL TODAY!" and sported a swastika.

"That," said Steve, "is some sick shit. Rambla, would you pee on that fence, please?"

For the moment, Skip forgot about the pink-haired kid's sudden bolt. "Oh, man! You won't believe this woman I met yesterday." She wasn't supposed to talk to Steve about cases (although she did), but for some reason she couldn't stand to tell him about the wall of epithets. She wanted to get Emily Martinez off her chest, though. "She was pissed because the tenant who got killed in her illegal Airbnb unit was Hispanic. Said if we only had Americans here, we wouldn't have these kinds of problems."

He nodded. "I've heard that one."

"Well, here's the kicker. Guess what her last name was? Martinez!"

Steve snorted. "I think I'm going to go out in the woods and meditate. Rambla, want to come with me?"

"You know what you should do your next film about? This! This kind of crap."

"What? Hatespeak?"

"Yeah. As the new 'Free Speech Movement'."

"Wouldn't be surprised if somebody else already has that covered — I bet it's got a dozen filmmakers working on it as we speak."

"I just want to understand it! I mean, these guys — you know, the ones that demonstrate in their baseball helmets and gas masks? With their bats and their homemade wooden shields? Like they've improvised some half-baked comic book super-hero kids' costume. Do they think they're in junior high or what? What kind of cowboys-and-Indians thing is that?"

"I think," Steve said, "That you mean cowmen and Native Americans."

ody had liked the cop — both cops, actually. She was a little intimidated by the one they called A.A. — most of the men she'd known had been dangerous — but he was the exact image she had in her head of what a dad might be like. A really nice dad. He'd tried to turn away from her, but she'd seen his eyes go wet when she talked about her fear.

Skip was Melody's pal and for an adult she'd been pretty great. Not condescending, not demanding — she'd just let Cody tell her story. And Cody knew Skip had the dog brought in just for her. She tried to pretend otherwise, but Cody could tell. That was really nice of her.

The only thing you could say about Melody was, she was awesome. Maybe Cody could still trust her, but she wasn't sure.

The question was, trust her for what? She couldn't know she'd be safe at Covenant House. Because that cop shop was a vipers' nest, and she didn't know how much Melody knew. Or how far they'd go to keep their dirty secrets.

Everything was okay till she went to the bathroom. She

and Melody were walking along just fine, friendly and everything, when she heard somebody say the N-word. It shocked her so much she turned around to see where it came from.

Two cops were walking towards them from another corridor — white cops — big guys with big shoulders and big bellies, both of them, one with a bunch of keys hanging from a belt loop, so he looked like some kind of jailer, the other wearing sunglasses. The one who'd said the word was telling a joke, something like, "A Jew, a N———, and a liberal walk into a bar…"

She didn't hear any more because of the shock waves reverberating through her system. She felt as if all the blood was draining from her head… but she knew she couldn't faint. She had to get away fast, before he saw her — or maybe he'd already seen her, she couldn't tell because of the sunglasses. But he and the other cop had passed quickly through Cody and Melody's corridor and continued along their own, so if he had, he'd only gotten a glimpse.

As soon as she was sure she wasn't going to faint, she sprinted to the rest room without a word to Melody, locked herself in a stall, and tried to think, her pulse pounding in her head, thoughts flying in all directions, sweat starting to pour. And suddenly she felt sick.

Sick! That was the answer. Sick would do it. She began to cough as if vomiting, dropped to the floor like someone hugging the toilet to hit the target, and even stuck fingers down her throat to get a realistic sound. After a good couple of minutes of retching, she flushed and opened the door to face Melody, who said, "You okay baby? You look like you've seen a ghost."

"I don't feel so good." Cody went to one of the sinks and rinsed out her mouth, as if she'd really just vomited, blood still racing, the panic as strong as ever, trying to think clearly. She couldn't really focus on anything but one overriding thought — she had to get out of here — now! "Can you take me home?" she asked. "I mean, back to the... you know... the house?"

"Sure," said Melody.

Cody waited till they got to a place where the traffic was bad and Melody wouldn't be able to maneuver in a hurry. As soon as they stopped at a light, she unbuckled her seatbelt, hopped out, left the door wide open, and took off running.

Running for her life, she was pretty sure.

Skip might have a cute dog, and A.A. might be the perfect dad and all, but they were still cops. No way in hell was she ever going to convince them of what she'd just found out.

The whale was a cop — maybe even a Homicide cop.

THE THING WAS, the kid had been their best lead. If they could have gotten an artist's sketch of the whale, it really would have helped. At least now they had a description — tall, thickly built, heavily muscled, shaved head, no tattoos the kid could remember, and dark but probably white.

"Fair enough assumption, considering he's a racist," said Cindy Lou Wootten, the department's sometime psychologist. "Funny about the tattoos," she said. "Guys like that usually have them. It's part of that hyper-masculinity thing they cultivate."

"What makes you think he's a racist?" A.A. said.

"Very funny," Skip said perfunctorily. "Well, according to Dia, he didn't take off his clothes. He could have plenty of tattoos we don't know about."

"He could be an athlete," Abasolo said. "He kind of sounds like Will Smith, by build anyway — not the movie star, the Saint who got shot. He sometimes had hair, sometimes not."

"And Will Smith was black," Cindy Lou reminded him. "Not exactly black like me — but black."

"Interesting point," Abasolo said, "that Dia wasn't sure he was white. That could describe half the people in this town. Not to mention Dia herself."

"Actually," Skip said, "her description fits at least three detectives in this division."

"Yeah, a drawing would sure have been nice. So where do we go from here?"

"Well, I'm no profiler," Cindy Lou said, "but we've now had two incidents a month apart — Sheba and Benny. But Benny was an interruption — the freak wanted to kill... well, Dia. Or whoever she was standing in for. I think he killed the next victims — at the Martinez house — because he had to kill someone. He couldn't wait for the right date. So what does that mean? He'll go for it next time?"

"If so, that theoretically gives us a minimum of 23 days to get him before he does it again. We can put the word out on the street to the ladies of the night and their gentlemen business managers. They're the ones at risk."

"Too bad they don't have a newsletter," Skip said.

"Hey, you know what? Let's talk to vice. Bet they've got websites. And Facebook pages. That's a start."

"Great idea! I've talked to the commander. No way we're going to get a task force till we get another — 'incident,' she called it. I said, 'flaying, you mean,' and she gave me the stinkeye. So we've got to be pretty resourceful."

"Do we believe Dia, by the way?"

"I believe her," Skip said. "The evidence lines up with

what she said." She shrugged. "Actually, she pretty much told the story we'd already told ourselves. The Benny theory makes sense if the whale killed him because Benny could identify him. Dia had his knives — we know that for a fact because they were found exactly where she said she put them — so he had to kill Benny some other way. But what about Miguel? Dia didn't think the whale knew him. Why'd he get killed?"

"Different m.o. entirely," Cindy Lou said. "Could be a coincidence."

"Didn't your mother mention there are no coincidences?" asked A.A.

"She just told me to beware of smart-talking white dudes." She gave him a flirtatious half-smile, which Skip noticed he returned.

"She was right too," he said. "How about the vacation rental companies?"

Skip said, "What do we tell them to look out for? Fake names? Can't think of a way for them to see this coming. Renters could be more careful, though. Hey, let's at least work on that one — we can get the famous Sergeant McPherson McAvoy on it. He's already sent out Dia's picture for tomorrow, by the way."

"Think that puts her in danger?" Abasolo asked.

Skip shrugged. "Lloyd's in jail, and Miguel's dead. The whale already knows she exists and what she looks like. So I don't think so — she'll be safest with us."

"Okay then," Abasolo said, "Russian roulette it is."

"Ooooh. Don't say that. Do you think I was wrong?"

"Naaah. We need to find her family somehow. Or some kind of history on her — 'cause somebody's got to take care of her. It's probably our best chance to keep her out of foster care." He paused, thinking about her. "Jeez, what a nightmare — two years in slavery, followed by...who knows what? We need to get her back to something familiar to her. Poor kid deserves a chance!"

Cindy Lou steered the conversation back on track. "But about McAvoy."

"Well, nothing's wrong with expanding the Airbnbad story. That part came out when Benny was murdered. Hey, I've got an idea — forget McAvoy. Our friend Jane Story's over at Channel 6 these days. We can always call her directly and mention the new victims were in a short-term rental as well. But if he strikes once a month, everybody's going to forget about it before the crucial time."

"Not necessarily. Maybe he books in advance. Also, maybe he's tried booking other places and the owners were suspicious and turned him down. They might know something. I think it's a good idea. I kind of feel like the more publicity on this one the better. So long as nobody mentions the wall of epithets. Or that Dia's a witness — McAvoy's press release just said she was a missing juvenile."

"I told Emily Martinez to keep her mouth shut, but she's not going to listen." Her phone rang. "Coroner," she told the others. She answered, listened, and reported.

"Cause of death is as expected — the guy was stabbed, the woman stabbed a lot, and a little bit at a time. In other words, tortured."

"Oooh." Cindy Lou sounded like she'd gotten the wind knocked out of her.

"All personal objects stolen — wallets, purses, licenses, all that. But they I.D.'d the bodies from fingerprints. Jimmy's emailing those now. So let's see what we can reel in. I'm calling Jane. And then we can go out and visit these people's friends. Unless something better turns up."

ALL CODY COULD THINK ABOUT WAS how to lose her hair. Even Melody had said it — it was how the cops found her. It was what made her stand out in a crowd and what she needed most to do was disappear. She wasn't about to go to a hairdresser, though. That was just leaving a wide-open trail.

The answer was to do it herself. But where and how?

Well, aside from Maw-Maw and Terry — and Zachary, of course — she only knew two people in the world who weren't criminals, cops, or friends of cops — Elliott and Mikey from the Clover Grill. She pulled out the now-tattered card Elliott had thrust upon her. Mikey lived with his parents, she remembered — they probably wouldn't appreciate a bedraggled kid showing up on their doorstep. It would have to be Elliott.

She looked at his card. The restaurant where he worked was in the French Quarter. That part was good, but the card also had his cell number — better still. She phoned.

"Hi, this is Cody from the other night. Remember me? The Pomeranian?"

"Yeah, sure, Coe, how're you doing? What's that about a Pomeranian?"

"You said you wouldn't abandon a Pomeranian, so you'd help me too."

He laughed. "Really? I said that? You were in pretty big trouble, babe. How'd it work out?"

"Not that great. My friend had a handsy boy friend." She didn't mention she'd also stolen money from her friend — she was so ashamed of that she might never mention it to anyone. "Hey, can we talk? I know this is weird, but I need a place to cut my hair. Any way you could... I don't know, maybe lend me some scissors? And a bathroom?"

He laughed. "You know what? You are a never-a-dull-moment kind of chick. How soon do you need it?"

"Umm... yesterday?"

"Let me think. I'm at work. You caught me on a break."

"Oh. I'm..."

"No, it's okay. Let me get right back to you."

"Sure." She felt deflated. She had no idea what "right back" might mean. It could be hours, she realized. Maybe he couldn't talk again till after his shift. Or maybe he was calling the cops. Or even the whale.

She was hanging out by the river — somehow it just seemed safer than the French Quarter proper — and she knew all about it from hanging there with Mikey and Elliott. Here she was free to do pretty much anything she wanted with no one noticing much, and certainly not caring. So she paced. Like some kind of maniac. She'd go twenty steps and then twenty steps back, thinking it would release tension, but all it really did was make her feel silly.

She was just sitting down on a bench, thinking to watch the river instead, when Elliott called back. "Where are you?"

"French Quarter."

"Good. So is Mikey. Can you meet him in ten minutes? He's at Dumaine and Chartres."

A wave of gratitude swept over her. "Wow, Elliott. Thanks so much for this."

"You know what?" he said, "I've been where you are."

Bet you haven't, she thought, but she appreciated the sentiment.

She got to the appointed corner in eight minutes flat and saw no sign of Mikey. Why, she wondered, had he chosen this corner? And then she heard him calling her. "Coe! Up here!" He was luxuriating on a lounge on the balcony across the street, barefoot and wearing shorts and sunglasses, like it was the middle of July. He was sipping a cocktail, his red hair sticking up like Woody Woodpecker's. He got up and leaned over the rail. "Come on over. I'll come down and get you."

The house was a plain-looking one, painted gray and off-white, no contrasting shutters and door, but it had an expensive-looking knocker on it. High-pitched barking accompanied Mikey's deft footsteps.

"Hey, baby," he said as he opened the door to a narrow outdoor passageway, the outer wall planted with ferns in hanging pots or stuck to pieces of wood. Already it seemed like some sort of mysterious hideaway.

An entire posse of tiny fluffy dogs jumped up and down behind him, seemingly whipped into a frenzy by the prospect of entertaining Mikey's pink-haired guest. "The guys and gal are friendly," Mikey said. "You like dogs?"

"Oh, sure," she said, thinking of Rambla, who, in contrast to these guys, seemed a paragon of canine calm. "Is this where you live?"

"Ha! No, my parents live in Metairie. Pretty tame for me, so this is heaven. My friend Marda's in Italy for a few weeks — how cool is that? So I'm housesitting. Come on in and check it out. Marcia, can y'all shut up?" Cody assumed he was talking to the dogs, but they continued barking, anyhow.

To their left was the house, and straight ahead was a courtyard bounded by some kind of outbuilding. Mikey headed that way. "Behold my kingdom," he said, hands out to the side like a Broadway musical star, and it was something to behold — a little tropical paradise complete with a fountain and tiny fish pond, palms, banana trees, bromeliads, and a perfect little seating area furnished with lacy, antique-looking cast-iron furniture. "Shall we perch here?"

Cody perched, but her insides felt squishy for some reason. She realized she was afraid in a weird way, terrified that she didn't deserve this, that it would be snatched away, that she was the nothing Miguel had told her she was for the past two years, a piece of human flotsam undeserving of a few minutes in a beautiful garden. She kept her eyes down for a moment, struggling to get control.

Mikey said, "What's the matter, dawlin'? You look like someone who's being chased."

As if on cue, one of the dogs leapt into her lap and began to snuggle down, perfectly confident of being welcomed there. Cody couldn't help, it, she laughed, running her hands through the thick honey-colored fur, and felt okay again. Well, as okay as she ever felt these days.

"That's Marcia Ball," Mikey said, "And you just passed a big test. If Marcia likes you, you can stay here. You still need a place?"

"What?" Cody couldn't believe what she was hearing. "I could stay here?"

"Look, I'm not going to ask too many questions, but I'd kind of like to know one thing — how old are you? About seventeen?"

"Yes," Cody lied. "I'll be eighteen in August."

"So sixteen," Mikey said. "If that. Don't look so surprised, I know that game. I've played it too."

"But you don't really know me," Cody said, "Why would you let me stay here?"

"Because people helped me when I needed it," he said, "and I've almost never seen anyone who needs help as bad as you do. Look, you're sixteen, you just blew into town, your only friend's a stripper, and you need to look different. Why do people need to look different? So they can't be recognized, that's why. And yet, you claim to only know one person in town. Who's gonna recognize you? There's a lot of story there that I don't know." He leaned back, obviously inviting her to tell it.

But she couldn't. She couldn't talk about being sold by her mother and trafficked to Houston and pimped out. Not again, not after telling Maw-Maw and Melody, and then the cops. Just. Could. Not. But maybe she could hit a couple of high points. "Something bad happened to me," she said, "and I fought back. That's where I was when I met you. Would you believe this? I thought I'd killed somebody!"

Mikey looked alarmed. "You kiddin' me?"

"He was trying to kill me. He was a... a freak. You know what I mean?" What she meant was "freak" in the way sex workers used the word — a way, she hoped, of letting him know exactly what had happened without having to come out and say she was turning a trick.

"Wooo. Girl!" he said.

"You know the next part — I ended up spending the night with my friend, and her boy friend nearly raped me. So I left there and..." she considered telling him about her days with Maw-Maw, but decided against it, "... in the end I went to that place where you told me to go."

"I told you to go somewhere? I don't remember that." But he looked slightly sly, as if he was testing her.

"Covenant House," she said. He nodded approvingly, letting her know she'd passed the test. "They were real nice to me there. And, finally, I went to the cops."

"Seriously? The cops?"

Yeah, because I thought a gang of pimps might be coming after my grandmother and also there's this killer it turns out I didn't actually kill. And he might be kind of mad.

"Well, the Covenant House people have good contacts with this cop on the case, and they convinced me they were already looking for me — and knew I didn't do it." She nodded, to emphasize she was telling the truth. "But while I was there, I saw him."

"What? You saw who?"

"The guy I thought I killed. He's a freaking cop!"

Very deliberately, Mikey turned forty-five degrees, and flicked his glance back at her. "You see that?" he said. "When they actually turn sideways, that's not just side-eye, that's Super Serious Side-eye. And that's what I'm giving that one. You know how preposterous it sounds, right?"

Cody could feel her whole body deflate, shoulders first. "Yeah. I do. That's why I ran away. Nobody's gonna believe me — ever. I am. So. Fucked."

Mikey surprised her by laughing. "Yeah, I kind of see your point. Nobody in hell's gonna buy that one. But that's why I'm helping you, right? Because you've got nowhere else to go?"

Cody felt such a surge of hope she almost smiled. "You mean you believe me?"

"Ummm... not exactly. I'm not gonna lie, I'm not sure what's going on here. But you're still a scared kid and I feel ya. You know? I've been there. And to tell you the truth, I'm in a little over my head here. I've got to go to work pretty soon and these guys have to be fed... and walked... and you, know... loved. And some of them have to have meds. I don't think I had any idea how much work four Pomeranians could be."

"What did you just say?"

"I said you're sketchy as hell, but you can stay here if you'll help me with the lady and gentlemen."

"I mean what did you call them? These are Pomeranians?"

"Yeah. Why?"

For the first time since she could remember, she laughed like she meant it. "It's what you and Mikey said that first night — that y'all would help a Pomeranian, so you'd help me."

"Yeah, well. That was before I knew I was allergic to them."

"Are you serious? You're allergic?"

"Yeah. And Marda's not due back for two weeks. So here's the deal — you sleep in the slave quarters and the dogs sleep with you. I can't let them in with me or I stop breathing. And they keep me up all night scratching on the door." He looked sheepish. "I've been here two nights and had to give them Zyrtec to put them to sleep, but I can't keep doing that — you know? They'd be little furry addicts by the time Marda gets back."

"I can do that," she said. "I'd love some dogs to sleep with."

"I'm sure gonna miss that pretty pink hair. You want to see your quarters? And then I'll cut it for you."

The slave quarters — or perhaps it had been a kitchen, Mikey said — who really knew? — had a narrow living room downstairs and a tiny bedroom and bath up a spiral staircase. And that was it. "No kitchen?" Cody asked.

"Why? You a gourmet cook?"

"I just thought... now that everybody's doing Airbnb..."

"Omigod! Airbnb! You know how dangerous that is these days? Some Airbnb tenant was killed the other day..."

Cody just stared at him.

He said, "What? You gonna faint or something?"

"You saw that on the news?"

"Are you kidding? Pretty hard to miss. Happened at a yoga studio. 'The Namaste Killer', they're calling him. Of course something like that's gonna make news."

"Mikey. That was January 2, right? The day of the Sugar Bowl. And the night you met me. Does that tell you anything?"

"Should it?"

"That's where I'd just come from. That guy, the one they found in the yoga studio, is who the cop killed."

Mikey hesitated only a minute. "Miss Thing, you've sure got an active imagination. What kinda haircut you want?"

But Cody had seen him take it in — she knew he was entertaining the possibility she could be for real. For now it didn't matter. He didn't care, and that was almost better.

15

"I don't know," she said. "It's not enough just to get the pink out, I've got to... you know... transform. Be somebody else."

"Did you say transform? What an interesting idea! How about if you transition instead?"

"What's that mean?"

"Girl friend! Where have you been?"

You can't even imagine, she thought. "Seriously, I've never heard that."

"Well, here's the short version — what if we turn you into a boy?" He assessed her chest, though not at all the way she was used to it being assessed. "Hmmm... you're skinny enough. We could get you an Ace bandage for the melons."

She laughed. "More like lemons."

"My point exactly."

Cody found the idea not just appealing, but something of a life raft. Not to be herself was the immediate goal, but not even to be female — after what she'd been through — was plain lagniappe.

Mikey took her over to the Big House and sat her on the side of the bathtub.

And without the slightest twinge of regret, she watched him cut off her foot-long, pink-tipped tresses, and smiled as he buzzed her head with a razor. She really did look different. About eleven years old, for one thing.

"I guess you're a boy," he said, "But you sure are nellie. Maybe some glasses..."

He found a pair of black-framed ones and slipped them over her nose. "Oh, no way. These look like Halloween Groucho Marx ones."

"Hat?" she suggested.

"Definitely not a baseball cap. You'd look like you were on a girls' softball team. How about a fedora?" He produced a narrow-brimmed one. "Not bad. Maybe with a pair of shades..."

"Hey, that's it! I'm a junior high hipster." She knew the get-up wouldn't fool anyone for long, but at least she looked different from a distance.

He opened the medicine cabinet and pulled out an Ace bandage. "You can add this when you go out. And my T-shirts will fit you. What do you think?"

"I think you're... my bestie!" she cried, and hugged him impulsively. She never did things like that. I must be excited, she thought. I must think I'm going to live.

After a moment's hesitation, he hugged back. "Okay, then. Make your boobs disappear, and let's walk the kids — you take two and I'll take the other two. And then I'm off to impersonate a mixologist. Oh, hey, if we meet anybody, what's your new name?"

She thought about it. "How about C.T? Those are my initials."

"I like it. It's unisex. Doesn't bring up embarrassing questions."

As it happened, they did meet someone — multiple someones — one of Mikey's friends, a couple of Marda's neighbors — and half a dozen people who just wanted to pet an entire pack of perfectly groomed fluffy little dogs. No one even looked twice at Cody.

Mikey shrugged. "Well, this is the French Quarter. I could wear a dress and a pair of flippers on my feet and no one would bat an eye. An epicene teen-ager is pretty tame for these here parts." He paused, considering. "On the other hand, you know what? Who looks at humans when Pomeranians are around? I think that's it, C.T., old chap! Just be sure you always have a couple of dogs with you, and you're golden."

Once the pack was walked and fed, and Mikey had gone off to impersonate a mixologist, Cody spent an hour composing a text to Maw-Maw. She wanted to reassure her and yet warn her — no easy task. Finally, she gave up on subtlety and just came out and said it: I'm safe, but I need to make sure you are too. Have to stay away for now. Best if you don't know where I am. Miss you and love you so much!

She found that walking the dogs had cleared her head as much as a good night's sleep. She knew exactly what to do next.

Despite herself, she couldn't get the image of the whale out of her head, striding the corridors of police headquarters in a suit and tie like he owned the place. And wearing those shades! She hoped he was wearing them because he was now blind in one eye, thanks to her.

During the walk, the desperate urge to draw — in fact to draw a particular face — had become almost overwhelming.

Her best subject had always been art and she'd missed it like crazy while she was a captive.

When they returned to Marda's, she asked Mikey for drawing paper and pencils, but the best he could come up with was a lined legal tablet. That was good — lots of pages to screw up. The floor was littered by the time she was done. She'd drawn him as she last saw him — in suit, tie, and shades. Looking exactly like a cop.

Before she had time to change her mind, she photographed the drawing and texted it to Melody, with a note: "This is the whale. Show Skip."

And then she sent it to Maw-Maw as well: "Run like hell if you see this man. No matter who he says he is, DON'T talk to him. Love, C."

After that, she took a luxurious bath, no quick showers for C.T., and called her furry friends to join her in bed: "Marcia Ball! Dr. John! Andy J. Forest! Washboard Chaz!"

St. Anthony's Gardens had been great and Covenant House perfectly okay, but nothing, absolutely nothing could compare to snuggling with what Mikey called The Chartres Street Quartet. Cody just called them Marcia and the band.

She would have slept long and late if it hadn't been for the Quartet making morning music, the real reason, she surmised, that Mikey wouldn't sleep with them. "Let us out, you lie-abed," they yipped. "Feed us, serving wench! Need to pee, worker bee!" They had quite the vocabulary when demanding services.

Bleary-eyed and woozy, she stumbled out to the courtyard to enable their majesties to answer their various calls of nature, in the process finding a note taped to the door of her outbuilding. Hello, Dia Boudreaux, you big liar! You've got a phone, right? You need to text me the number. Meanwhile, check out nola.com on my iPad— look on the kitchen table."

She was mortified. Not to mention terrified. What on earth could nola.com have to say about her?

Mikey'd left his tablet open to the news site. And there she was — Dia Boudreaux, missing juvenile. Has anyone seen her? the caption asked. Cody couldn't believe it. The drawing was so good, it practically spoke — and what it said was, "Help me!" She thought it must have been done from a surveillance tape at police headquarters. But in that case, why not just use the photo? she wondered. Along with wondering if she'd really looked that pitiful just yesterday.

And then it hit her — it had come from surveillance tape, all right, but not yesterday. Very likely it was from January 2, somewhere on Magazine Street, the night Benny got killed. It was probably what the cops had sent to Covenant House that enabled Tracy to recognize her.

Cody couldn't stop staring. In a way the drawing gave her hope, made her look at her life in perspective. She could see at a glance how far she'd come. She wondered if it was obvious to others, not just herself, that, regardless of the makeover, she was no longer the same person she'd been a week ago. Her confidence was coming back; her sense of self.

If I live through this, she thought with amazement, I think I'm going to be okay.

≈

ABASOLO ARRIVED at Homicide five minutes after Skip did — having stopped to get Skip a skinny vanilla latte, as well as a more muscular tall dark roast for himself. "Just checked the tip line," she said. "Got a message from a Chantelle

Thibodeaux saying the pseudonymous Dia Boudreaux is her granddaughter, Cordelia Thibodeaux, aka Cody."

Abasolo grinned. "Okay, I see how the kid came up with that one. Boudreaux, Thibodeaux, what's the difference? Tell me everything."

Instead, Skip sipped her latte. "This is so good."

"I love it when you do that."

"Do what?"

"That little moaning sound you make. That's really why I get you the coffee."

"Sexist." But she had to laugh. She suspected she blushed slightly as well.

"So what's Chantelle's story? Have you talked to her yet?"

Skip nodded. "Yeah. Sounds like a nice lady, but she's pretty messed up about the kid." She shrugged. "Her story's exactly the same as Dia's. The mom selling her, the trafficking to Houston, the whole thing."

"Whoa! How does she know all that? Because if it's true, she wouldn't have seen the kid in two years. "

"It seems Cody went home before ending up at Covenant House."

"Where's home?"

"Houma. She stayed with Chantelle for two days, then did a bunk. Just like here. And last night she texted that she was safe, but her grandmother might not be."

Abasolo nodded. "She might be right. Pretty sure Miguel and Lloyd weren't acting alone. The FBI's on that — sweating Lloyd and cooperating with the Houston P.D. Smart kid. If they knew the mom's name and location, they could go looking for... hmmm... guess we're going to have to call her Cody. And if they were looking for Cody, they'd try to squeeze Chantelle."

"There's something else, A.A. Got bad news for you. Real bad."

"Fuck! They already got to her?"

"Worse. Cody sent her a drawing with a warning. She also texted it to Melody, to show us." She handed her phone to Abasolo.

"Holy double shit!" He looked around in a panic. "Let's get out of here."

She gave a quick nod. "Totally with you."

They didn't speak again till they were in Skip's car. "Let me see that thing again," A.A. said. "Am I seeing what I think I'm seeing?"

"I'm seeing Fazzio. Exactly the way he looked yesterday. She must have seen him at headquarters. That's why she split."

"Yeah. Maybe on the way to the bathroom. We could ask Melody when she first said she was sick."

"You know what everyone says about Fazzio. That he looks exactly like some Saint."

Abasolo nodded, messing with his phone. "James Forbes. He's a tight end. Take a look at this."

"You've gotta be kiddin' me!" She was staring at a picture of a hairless man in a football uniform. "What, are they twins?"

"Now that I think of it, Fazzio's got a look. A lot of guys look like that. Really buffed out, shaved head..."

"Mean expression."

"You said it, not me. So we're not really discussing whether the guy who just killed three people — a suspected serial killer-to-be — is either a guy we work with or a well-known sports figure?"

Skip's stomach felt shaky. She wanted to say, "Right. Let's

just pretend none of this ever happened." But she forced herself to say, "What do we know about Forbes?"

"You really think we should talk about that first? We have an I.D. from a witness."

She made herself take it in. That was exactly what they had. "Okay, you go first. How well do you know Fazzio?"

"Not that well. You?"

"Same. He's a decent cop. Right?" Skip didn't like Chris Fazzio, but didn't want to say so. Right now she was feeling oddly defensive towards him.

Abasolo said, "I guess. I don't think he's got any kind of record of violence or anything. Have you worked with him?"

She finally blurted, "I may as well say it. He's a bully. Sexist as hell. The kind of cop who kicks suspects. Especially..."

Abasolo saw where she was going. He finished for her. "Especially if they're black."

"Boy, I hate this conversation! What about Forbes?"

Abasolo googled. "Oh, boy... a woman he dated said he hit her."

"Yeah? Black or white?"

"Black. And I'm pretty sure Forbes is white. But he didn't really hit her, he just shoved her. Here's the video. Claimed it was an accident."

Skip watched the video. "It doesn't look like an accident."

"So is he a suspect too?"

"I just... don't know. Damn! We've got to find Cody."

"Hey! She sent you the drawing, right? We can text her."

"No, she sent it to Melody. And also her grandmother. But sure, one of them could text her."

Abasolo raised an eyebrow. "Hey, what's up with Fazzio's shades? Eye injury, by any chance?"

"You know what? He was out most of the week. Could be."

"We'll have to bring the commander in on this — we can ask then. But yesterday was his first day back, and he wore those shades all day."

"I don't want to do anything in the office. You know? I wonder if we can get the commander to meet us somewhere."

"Boy, she's gonna hate that!"

"She's gonna hate all of it," Skip said. "Tell you what, let's put it off for a little while. Why don't we split these guys up and see if we can eliminate either or both of them before we talk to her?"

Abasolo didn't waste a second. "I'll take Forbes."

"Kinda thought you were gonna say that."

"You know it's the right thing. We guys do better with the sports talk."

"Go knock it out of the park, hot shot. I'm going to work in my car for a while. Too many ears in that building."

Abasolo grinned. "I hear ya. So to speak."

CODY SAW MAW-MAW HAD CALLED, but she wasn't going to listen. Just couldn't. It was too painful to hear her voice.

She'd texted too: Come home, my darling girl! We'll take care of you, I promise we will.

Cody shook her head, thinking, She doesn't get that it's not me I'm worried about.

She wrote, I love you, Maw-Maw! and then texted Mikey a note setting the record straight, Not Dia Boudreaux! At least not Boudreaux. Dia was one of my nicknames as a baby, but everyone calls me Cody now. Just wanted you to know, I did lie — but not to you! Sincerely, Cordelia Thibodeaux.

For good measure, she also sent her drawing of the whale: If you see this guy, run like hell!

Careful not to wake her host, she fed the dogs and took them to Jackson Square, where the artists and Tarot readers were just setting up for the day. She was particularly taken by the artists. Some painted French Quarter scenes, some musicians, some did caricatures... all things she could do, she was pretty sure.

She could feel her talent rising up inside her like the Kundalini energy one of her fellow captives had talked about. As Cody understood it, that was something coiled at the base of the spine like a snake, and it could rise up your spine and explode out your head if you weren't careful. That was what this felt like.

During her two years of horror, she'd had to live in neutral, feeling as little as possible, thinking not at all, and never doing anything except what she was ordered to do. Now she wanted to experience life, to accomplish something. After drawing the whale — he'd really come out great, she thought — she wanted to draw a lot more. She wanted that desperately.

And she felt so free in her new persona. She sat on a bench for a while to watch men, observing the way they walked, the way they sat, the way they stood. Surreptitiously, she practiced man-spreading, finally leading the dogs away, walking like a boy — shoulders slightly hunched, legs a bit apart, barely picking her feet up. She found if she imagined herself as Godzilla, she automatically held her hands slightly out from her sides, like she'd seen men do in fights, and slowed her gait, making each step deliberate and a little menacing, thus becoming (in her mind) larger and more intimidating. If she was going to be a boy, she might as well be a scary one.

By the time she got Marcia and the band back home, Cody had another voice message — this one from the cop. Damn! Melody had obviously given her the number. Well, she should have expected that. This one she listened to:

Cody, this is Skip Langdon. I've talked to your grandmother. She said to say she loves you and wants you to come home. But I'm calling because I want you to know we're taking your information VERY SERIOUSLY. I completely understand why you left yesterday. We need your help in the investigation. Can you call me, please?

Ha! thought Cody. In a pig's eye. Or maybe when pigs fly. And then she remembered "pig" was a pejorative for "cop" and thought with pleasure that she'd been able to make an unconscious pun because of the reawakening she was experiencing. Energy was coursing through her.

She felt joyful! Sure, someone was out to kill her, but it wasn't Miguel and she didn't have to give some repulsive drunk a blow job ever again. She had a friend and a great place to stay and four dogs to love. She was going to live to the max!

She went to Wal-Mart for supplies. There she bought a sketch pad, an entire set of artist's pencils "for beginners" for only $17, a backpack (boys all seemed to have them), and some clothes. First a sports bra — the Ace bandage was killing her. Then, a boy's white button-down shirt and a pre-tied tie that snapped in back, a black T-shirt, black boys' skinny jeans. She even used the men's dressing room. No one even looked twice.

Finally, she bought a new phone. She transferred Skip's, Maw-Maw's, and Melody's numbers and threw the old one in the river on the way home.

Mikey appeared in the courtyard around noon. "Hiya, C.T. Got your text. So you're still Cody? You are an extremely non-boring chick. One day you're going to have to tell me the story of your life."

"Hiya, Mikey! Yes, Cody at your service. The kids are all fed and walked and here's a present for letting me stay here." She proffered a newly drawn portrait of him, using her new colored pencils.

He studied it carefully. "Hey, you got my coiffeur just right! Am I a dead-ringer for Woody Woodpecker or what?"

She couldn't help laughing. She'd always thought that, but would have never said so to Mikey, even though the effect did seem deliberate.

"This is awesome. Why didn't you say you were so talented? Hey, where'd you get the art supplies?"

"Wal-Mart. Along with a bunch of new boy clothes — like this outfit?" She'd changed into the black jeans and black shirt. "And I learned how to walk." She did her impression of the sophomore shuffle she'd been practicing, and it was his turn to laugh.

"Hey, not bad. You look like every arrogant acne-covered adolescent asshole in New Orleans."

"I'm gonna take that as a compliment. Wanna see my man-spread?"

She demonstrated, even lightly shifting a pair of imaginary balls, and that tickled him even more. "So. An actress as well as an artist."

"Actor if you don't mind. I'm a boy." She gave him another drawing. "Here's one of Marcia and the band."

"Awesome possum! You even got Andy J.'s cowlick. Bet you could make a fortune at Jackson Square. No, wait. You have to get a license for that. The others would chase you away. Frenchmen St., though. Or Decatur."

"Really? Think I could?" She spread out a few more drawings she'd made — of just about every plant in the courtyard, plus vignettes of plant groupings, a panoramic view of the entire space, and a view of the river done from memory. "These are just rough. I did them in a hurry."

"Woo-hoo! America's got talent. Well, why don't you try it? You sure seem independently wealthy, but the boy drag had to set you back."

"You don't know the half of it — I even got a tie."

"You should wear that to sell. Everybody else just looks scruffy."

She didn't tell him, but that was why she'd bought it.

"Know what you should do? Go down to Kruz on Decatur and get some kind of cool Indian fabric thing to lay the art out on. Go out about 4 or 5, maybe even later. The crowds pick up then."

"Cool!" That would give her plenty of time to create a few more pictures.

16

Skip sat in her car for a while, trying to pull together everything she knew about Fazzio. She'd had an uneasy feeling talking to Abasolo, a kind of conflict. She should be loyal to Fazzio as her brother in blue, at least give him the benefit of the doubt. But the guy creeped her out; there was no getting around it. His neck and shoulders were huge, from working out. He walked like a gorilla, and deliberately, she thought. His shoes came down a little too hard, maybe even had some kind of taps on them, to make his footsteps sound ominous. He liked to be intimidating, wanted to be. But the department was full of guys like that.

That was just the start. She didn't even know how to explain it to a male colleague, but the guy was sexist as hell. If there were both sexes in a room, he'd ignore the women even if they spoke to him. She knew; he'd done it to her. He'd pretend not to hear them if they spoke up in a meeting, and speak over them. And then, five minutes later, he'd spew out what they said as if he'd thought of it himself. Did he do it to the commander? Yes! Now that Skip thought of it, she'd even seen that.

If she had to work with him — and Skip had only a few times — he'd try to take charge as if he were the ranking officer (although Skip outranked him), or as if it was his case when it was actually hers. He was a bully, too. She'd had to question witnesses with him more than once and found it a thoroughly unpleasant experience. He bullied them and her.

In short, he was nobody's idea of the stereotypical serial killer — the meek, friendly guy everyone said wouldn't hurt a fly. But he was her idea of a terrific candidate for one. The thought of him with that brave sixteen-year-old who'd been in her office yesterday sickened and frightened her. She could literally feel her flight-or-fight response gearing up, the blood starting to pound in her ears, her mouth going dry.

What all that meant, she thought, was that she had to be very, very careful. She couldn't let her animosity towards the man impair her judgment. She almost wished she'd asked for Forbes.

Who knew Fazzio well? she wondered. Maybe that was a place to start. He'd come to Homicide from Property Crimes, before that from the Third District. She had friends at the Third District.

She phoned and asked for Duck Duckworth, a detective about ready for retirement, she surmised — and somebody nothing got past.

"Well, Sergeant Langdon," he said, "you not so stuck up now you've made sergeant you don't have time for your old friends anymore?"

"Always time for you, Duckie. Let me take you to lunch."

Antennae went up immediately. "What you need?"

"You know. Usual thing. Just a little intel. Top secret classified eyes only."

"Ooooo. That deserves a drink. How about 5 p.m."

"Any way we could make it earlier? It's pretty urgent."

There was a pause. And finally, "I can sneak out at three."

"Coffee or alcohol? We need a cop-free zone."

"You kidding? Alcohol. How about Mid-City Yacht Club. They got a courtyard. We can be cloak-and-dagger as hell and nobody's gonna hear us unless you've got a bug in your bra."

"I try to avoid that. Some of them sting."

Duckworth was a skinny white dude with thinning sandy-gray hair, worn semi-long for a cop. He had a wiry gym-fit body clothes looked good on. At any rate, Skip always thought of him as dapper, not a word she applied to the average cop. Even Abasolo.

He was sitting in the courtyard of the neighborhood sports bar, already nursing a beer and looking utterly relaxed in khakis and a polo shirt. Skip said, "Hey, Dapper Dan. Looking good."

"Not as good as you, dawlin'. Beautiful day, ain't it?" He spread his arms as if to show her.

"Ducky, it's overcast as hell and the humidity's gotta be 95."

"I rest my case. It's January, Sergeant! Are we lucky or what? Other people got snow up to their ass."

"Yeah, you right, Ducks. I must be in a bad mood."

"Well, hell. Let me buy you a beer. Beer cures all ills."

"Naaah, I might have to work late. I need to ask you some confidential stuff. Really really confidential. You up for that?"

"Baby, I'd love to be your Deep Throat."

"I'm not going anywhere near that one."

"See, I can say it, but you can't, because if you do..."

"Yeah, I get it. Listen, it's about a detective you used to work with. Remember a guy named Fazzio?"

Duckworth set down his beer and gave her a full frontal stare. And then he whistled. "That guy."

She sighed. "I was afraid of that. Go ahead, tell me."

"What's this about? You get transferred to Public Integrity or what?"

That was the last thing she wanted to deal with. Public Integrity was NOPD's version of Internal Affairs. So it was a fair question, but she didn't want him thinking about what division she was actually in. No way she wanted it to get around that she was investigating a fellow officer for a homicide. She settled on a lie that was also the truth. "Nope. Still in the same old place. So far as I know Public Integrity's not after him. Just wondering about a couple of things. I thought maybe you could talk me through it."

He squinched up his eyes, clearly not believing her. "Okay, good enough. Why am I not surprised? You finding him a little disrespectful of our beautiful and shapely women in blue?"

"That's your cute way of saying do I find him sexist? Can we leave me out of it? Just wondering what they thought at the Third." She was being careful not to say she had personal issues with Fazzio. "How to say this? Let's try it this way — he's new at Homicide and we need to find the most constructive ways to work with our talented new colleague."

"Right. Talented. I'm not so sure about that. I even wonder why he became a cop. But you're sure being cagey."

She ignored that one. "Why wouldn't he become a cop?"

"Okay, Langdon, why'd you become one?"

She shrugged. "I'm a big ol' girl — I figured it was something I could do."

"But why'd you want to?"

"I don't know — adventure? Change of scenery every day?"

"All right, then, you're the exception. You know what most cops say?"

"Sure. They say they want to help."

"Now you got it." Duckworth took a healthy pull on his beer. "Far as I can tell Fazzio doesn't want to help anybody. He's the type of cop who kicks suspects when they're already disabled. Even if they're women. Especially if they're women." He paused, and Skip wondered if he was going to say, "or black."

"And you can guess what else," he said instead.

"Ummm.... let's see. Black?"

"Guy's a racist, no two ways about it. The captain couldn't wait to get him out of here."

Skip could just bet — the third District captain was African-American, female, and on the petite side. She'd hate Fazzio's way of looming like an ape even if it weren't for the more serious charges. "Aww, Ducky," she said. "Why mince words like that? Why not just come out with it?"

She was kidding, but he decided to take her literally. "Guy's a flaming asshole racist sexist sadist. Does that cover it?"

"So you don't find him at all creepy?" This time she was half kidding, half probing.

"Creepy. Funny you'd say that."

"Why?"

"He seemed to really get off on gruesome crime scene pictures. It was creepy as hell, now that you mention it."

"Oh, hell. Now you're scaring me."

He narrowed his eyes and leaned in close. "Be very

afraid," he said. He might have been kidding and he might not have.

She hadn't expected such an unmitigated portrait of a creep — and very likely a criminal. Well, obviously he was a criminal — a serial assailant if you counted kicking suspects who were already down. Sure, cops got away with it, but it was still assault. And cowardly, nasty, bullying assault in Skip's book. She was trying to take it all in.

But the whole portrait was so extreme it took her aback. She said, "Did the guy have any friends? Some fellow mean boys or something?"

Duckworth sucked beer again. "Yeah, he did have a friend. And no mean boy either. Gus Clarke. You know him? Good guy."

She did and she agreed. But one thing surprised her. Clarke was black. "What's up with that? If Fazzio's a racist?"

"Well, they're no longer friends," Duckworth said. "And I imagine thereon hangs a tale."

Skip couldn't wait to hear it. She stood and was about to say good-bye, but she didn't get that far. "What's going on?" Duckworth said. "The guy finally go ahead and commit a homicide?"

"Would it be okay," she said, "if you could just forget this conversation ever happened?"

He assumed an innocent expression. "What conversation?"

"You're okay, pal." She shook hands and left with kind of a warm glow — not so easy considering the chilling intel she'd just gathered. It was all about Duckworth. Guys like that made her feel proud to be a cop. There were some bad ones, sure, but Ducky Duckworth was old school — in a good way.

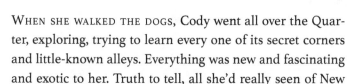

WHEN SHE WALKED THE DOGS, Cody went all over the Quarter, exploring, trying to learn every one of its secret corners and little-known alleys. Everything was new and fascinating and exotic to her. Truth to tell, all she'd really seen of New Orleans were the places she'd been to with her family, plus that awful motel, and the Wal-Mart.

She avoided Bourbon St. because of the traffic and the crowds — even in the daytime! — but mostly because of the smell. Usually it stank. And it was ugly. What a shame, she thought, that this was all so many tourists saw, when the rest of the French Quarter was so beautiful.

Mikey had warned her to stay mostly on the riverside of Bourbon, but she walked over to Dauphine St. sometimes in the part he told her was called "the lower Quarter", the side farthest from Canal St., which separated the French Quarter from what he called "the American sector". That made her laugh, even though he said it was really a thing. Something about the French being there first and then along came the crude and socially unacceptable "Americans", who settled on the other side of Canal. "Weren't the French Americans if they lived here?" she'd asked. And that prompted laughter on his part. Short answer: Definitely not. Just ask them.

Between Dauphine and Burgundy in the lower Quarter she'd discovered Cabrini Park, which seemed a kind of unofficial dog park. Although Mikey had warned that Marcia and the band were far too aristocratic to hang out with mere mutts, they did seem to like to watch them cavort and chase each other. So Cody would take them as far as the fence, where Dr. John nearly went crazy trying to squeeze between the bars and mix it up with the commoners. The others just watched attentively, with the dignity befitting their station as doggie royalty.

Sometimes she'd even take them to a park across Esplanade, outside the Quarter and deep in the Marigny.

She was leaving Cabrini Park the second day of her transformation (which Mikey still called her "transition"), when she spotted a familiar red mop atop a person with a familiar jaunty walk. A rush of regret and affection rolled over her so fast she didn't have time to think before she called out, "Terry!"

Her friend looked so confused she momentarily forgot she looked different now.

She took off the shades. "It's me, Cody." Seeing Terry's expression change to one of disdain, she followed up quickly. "I am so so sorry for what I did. You found the money, right? In your mailbox? That's what I came for that day — to return it."

"I trusted you. I let you in my house."

She didn't know what to say. What she'd done was inexcusable, but still... there was so much at play there. "I was a different person then."

A harsh sound that could have been a laugh came out of Terry. "That was less than a week ago!"

"Well... I'd been a prisoner for two years. I hadn't been around anyone who wasn't a criminal for a long time."

She could see Terry softening. She pressed her advantage. "Didn't you make any mistakes when you first got out?"

"Okay. Yeah. Some. Listen, I kind of understand, but Winston just doesn't. He has very strict standards where I'm concerned. Nobody messes with me, that's his attitude. He's so protective." She even gave Cody a half-smile.

"Well, I hope you know I'm grateful and I'd never do anything to hurt you."

"Thanks. Can I ask you a question — are you transitioning or something?"

"How does everybody know that word but me? I just needed to lose my hair, that's all. And then I got this idea." She indicated her transformed self. "In case Miguel and Lloyd's guys come after me."

Terry's face took on an enigmatic look. "Miguel's not coming, that's for sure!"

"Well, I..." she stopped, not sure she had the nerve to say it. But she managed. "I think I have you to thank for that. Don't I?"

The sphinx look twisted into something angry and a little dangerous. "What are you talking about?"

"I told you where he was. I mean... where he kept us. When I found out he was dead, I thought you probably..."

"Stop thinking," she said. "Now! You're crazy as hell, you know that?"

But Cody didn't think so. "No, no, you don't have to pretend. I just want to thank you for it. Miguel's never going to grab another girl again, and that's got to be good. And I'm never going to tell anybody."

"Are you crazy? I could never hurt another human being." Her eyes brimmed with makeup-ruining liquid. "Even Miguel."

Terry was about to brush past her, but Cody remembered something. "Terry?" she said. "I saw them take his body out. That's how I know what happened. And ever since then I've searched every online news site — TV and print both — for any mention of it at all, and ... nothing. How'd you know he was dead?"

"I heard it somewhere." She pushed past so fast she almost sent Chaz sprawling. Rocking back to his feet, the little dog huffed out a faint woof to express his displeasure.

Cody felt almost certain now. Before it had just been suspicion, based mostly on the card she'd noticed at Terry's apartment, the one for a gym with an underlined address on it. But if Terry knew Miguel was dead, either she'd done it or Winston had.

Because the address was for the Bayou Motel.

17

This time Skip won. She'd made a date for drinks with Gus Clarke and texted Steve that she wouldn't be home for dinner, since she and Abasolo had agreed to stay away from the office until they had a clearer idea of what they were looking at.

So now she was contentedly picking her way through the Hail Caesar salad at The Red Dog while Abasolo wrapped his slender frame around a Patty Melt that looked as if it could have beaten him in a wrestling match. He'd just delivered the news that Forbes had the alibi of the century. He and his family had left for Cancun and Tulum the second the Saints played their last game of the season — on December 28.

"The only thing even more iron-clad," Skip said "would be if he'd actually played a game the night Cody was assaulted — in front of the whole country."

"Yeah. Both the hotel and the airline vouched for 'em. They just got back yesterday. That lets Forbes out for Benny Solo as well as the murders at the lovely Emily's house. Oh, hey!" He reached for his phone. "We just got I.D.'s on those bodies — Jaime Schwartzkopf and Destiny Sinclair. Hmmm... Seems like there's some kind of irony to Destiny's name, but... maybe not. I mean everybody's got a destiny, right?"

Skip winced. "I think it would make me think twice about naming a kid that. Or an animal. And Jaime wasn't middle Eastern."

"Non sequitur, anyone? How'd you come up with that?"

"I was just remembering how Emily didn't think he was good enough to die on her floor. How does anybody tell what anybody is, anyhow?"

Abasolo said, "I've got a confession to make. I thought Jim Forbes was black till my buddy at the Saints office clued me in."

"He's white, right?"

"Yeah, just kind of dark. He's half-Italian, like me. Only the other half. My dad was Italian. His mom, I guess." He looked down at his knees for a moment. "So obviously we're putting off the inevitable. What did you come up with on Fazzio?"

"I hate to say it, but my buddy Duckworth..."

"Ducky Duckworth? Good man!"

"Well, he doesn't think Fazzio is. Know what his parting words were? He asked if the guy finally went ahead and committed a homicide."

"Oof." Abasolo set down his sandwich and slumped. "What's the problem?"

"Sounded like your basic anger issues, plus some down-home bigotry." She shrugged. "Nothing that couldn't apply to half the good ol' boys in Louisiana. Oh, but he also said the guy gets off on grisly crime pix."

"I know other cops like that. Don't you? Still, we've got a witness."

"If we could just find her. Let's see what Gus says. I told him 8 o'clock."

"Oh, good. We've got time for dessert."

After he'd polished off an order of cherry almond bread pudding (with a little help from his dining companion), they headed out to Lucky's Lounge in New Orleans East — Clarke's neighborhood — which he promised was guaranteed a hundred per cent cop-free (with three notable exceptions). He wasn't kidding.

Stiletto stares pinned them the second they walked in, but tensed shoulders descended when Clarke waved them to his table. Skip almost didn't recognize him. It had been a long time, and he'd shaved his head.

After greetings and drink orders, he said, "What can I do you for you guys? Pretty one-of-a-kind having a couple of Homicide cops ask for a secret meeting at a dive bar in the East."

"Here's to you," Abasolo said, and they clinked beer bottles.

"We hear," Skip began, "that you're the best guy to tell us about a guy in our department —"

"You gotta mean Chris Fazzio."

"We heard he was a friend of yours."

"I wouldn't exactly put it that way."

"Former friend?"

"Try close family member I had a falling-out with."

Abasolo literally scratched his head on that one. Skip took a moment to reconnoiter. "Ummm... how's that?" was the best she could do.

He put down his beer and gave them both a big grin, enjoying the sensation he'd created. Finally, he opened his palms in the "what-can-I-say" pose. "Simple," he said. "My Aunt Monica married his dad."

"Well," Skip managed, "tell us everything."

Clarke sipped again. "Pretty tall order."

"Start at the beginning. Who are these people?" This was so far from what she thought she knew she was having trouble keeping her cool.

"Pretty typical deal, really. Chris' mom died and his dad — Uncle Al to me — married her nurse. You know how that can happen?"

Abasolo nodded. "I've seen it."

"Oh, man. Chris never saw it coming. I didn't know him then, though — I just know what he told me later. Anyhow, his dad's a smart dude, but kind of quiet — teaches some kind of engineering at Tulane, and Aunt Monica's smart and kind of out there. And very very... hot."

"Ah," Skip breathed.

"Perfect fit?" Abasolo asked.

"Oh, man! That poor guy had no idea what he was getting into." He paused again, and once again Skip definitely got the idea he was enjoying himself.

"Which means?" she said.

"She's mean as a feral cat. Temper like a rattlesnake. But she'll premeditate too. Oh, yeah, she loves to premeditate. The stuff she did to him..."

"Chris' dad?"

"Oh, no. Chris. See, he really had a hard time with the whole thing. His mom dying, his dad marrying the nurse he had the hots for, maybe even her being black — later on, he sure had trouble with that one. But at the time, the two families were all lovey-dovey. This was quite a coup for a Johnson — that was my mom's family. They didn't have any money and the Fazzios did, thus no race issues there.

"But Chris never could stand her. He gave her every kind of trouble an eleven-year-old kid knows how to." He raised an eyebrow. "And she retaliated. Big-time. Oh, man, the things she did to that kid."

Skip didn't want to hear it. They'd landed once more smack in the middle of serial killer-land.

But Abasolo said, "What kinds of things?"

He laughed. "I remember her chasing him with a flyswatter one time."

"Ewww. But that doesn't really constitute torture, does it?"

"Hey, that's what we used to call her — Torture Mom. No, the flyswatter wasn't the torture. He was barefoot at the time and when he ran outside to get away, she locked the door on him. It was summer, and they didn't have a front yard or anything — there was just a sidewalk out there. You imagine how hot that was? She made him stay out there till his feet were good and blistered. You should have seen him hopping up and down."

"Oh, God." Skip put her head in her hands. Absolutely couldn't help it. "But why did the father let it happen?"

"Lord, he wasn't home. He never knew about half this stuff. When Chris would tell him, he'd say the kid was making it up."

"Did you see it?" Abasolo asked. "The flyswatter thing?"

Clarke nodded vigorously, and she saw that a kind of darkness had come over him. He was no longer enjoying himself. "Saw it. And heard it. I'm a year younger than Chris, and we were friends then — real good friends. My mom had left me there while she went and did something, so it was just the three of us. And I was used to Aunt Monica — real used to her. She told me to sit in a chair or she'd beat the crap out of me with that flyswatter. I had to listen to every damn thing she said to that poor kid."

"What did she say?"

He shuddered. "Nasty mean stuff. Stuff about how much it was gonna hurt — and how she was a nurse so she knew just what blisters did to your skin. And then she'd describe it and say she wasn't gonna treat the blisters, either, so maybe they'd get infected, and then she'd describe what that was gonna be like." He shuddered. "Meanest woman I ever saw in my life."

"Oh, boy," Skip said. "That could mess you up."

Abasolo said, "So — you two were close?"

"Actually, not so much then. I think we kind of resented being thrown together, to tell you the truth. But we were, a lot, from time to time. Even shared a room once. So we knew each other pretty well. Just used to fight a lot."

"Like kids do," Skip said.

"Pretty much." He said it as if not too sure, and Skip wondered if we was holding something back.

"Did you ever notice if he had any particular violent tendencies?"

Clarke twisted his face into a half-smile. "Well, we did have a cat that disappeared — that what you mean?"

But, having evidently heard her barely audible gasp, he quickly followed up with, "Naaaah. Just messin' with you. Pretty sure the stoopid cat just ran away. He could be mean, though. Not gonna lie to you, he was mean as hell at times..." he paused. "But, hell, we were kids. I was every bit as mean to him."

"What kind of mean?" Abasolo asked.

Clarke thought for a moment and shrugged. "Oh, just kid-mean, I guess. We were both selfish with our stuff and went out of control if the other one touched it."

Abasolo said, "Cost of living in a family."

"Yeah, I guess. We didn't really start to appreciate each

other till college. We both went to LSU and... you know how it is... he hung with the whiteys and I hung with the brothers. But then that first summer we started a business together, doing yard work for people. We did some good work." He took a satisfied drink and nodded, as if remembering once-happy times. "That's when we really got to be family in more than name only. We were like this." He made Velcro fingers.

"He got married, I got married, we both joined the department. You know what? We were each other's best man." He nodded again, like some ancient mariner dredging up a century-old memory. "Oh, man! Hard to believe now."

"What happened?"

"I'm gon' tell you what happened." This time he set his down his beer with a loud crack. Diminished as it was, a little spurted over the top. "This department's what happened. The guy started hangin' out with some of the wonderbread peckerwoods around here... yeah, I know that's not politically correct, but did you ever think that cuts two ways? If some of the Neanderthals around here think they can say the N word now that we got a neo-Nazi president, I don't see why I shouldn't call a nilla wafer a polar bear..."

It took Skip a minute to figure out what he was getting at, but Abasolo picked it up right away. "You mean like calling a spade a spade?"

Clarke made a finger gun, and took a shot at him. "You got it."

Skip started laughing. "Polar bear? Is that really a thing?"

"Oh, I've got a million of them — Casper, fish belly, Caucasoid... want me to go on?"

"No, I'm good." She had another laughing fit. "Fish belly?"

Abasolo snorted. "Guess we deserve it."

"Damn right you flatasses deserve it."

"Now, hold it," Skip said. "I do not deserve that one!"

Clarke and Abasolo looked at each other. "I'm not going near that," Abasolo said.

"Nooooo!" Clarke replied, and order was restored. "Well, anyway... lotta goddam racists in this outfit. Present company excepted. I hope."

"You bet," Abasolo said quickly.

Skip said, "Although everybody's..."

Clarke interrupted her. "Tha's right. Everybody is. So when Troy Weston was shot through the car window by one of our finest..."

"Ken Sullivan," Skip said. She remembered the case well. Although the kid he shot had no weapon, Sullivan had been exonerated of any crime.

"Yeah, well, I thought Sullivan shoulda fried."

Skip was beginning to get it. "And Fazzio disagreed."

"Yep. Pretty damn loud about it too. Guy went to bed one night and woke up a racist." He shrugged. "What can I say? We had a fight and that was it for us."

"What kind of fight?"

Clarke made a point of looking her straight in the eye. "Fisticuffs. The whole thing."

"How long ago was that?"

He looked off in the distance. "A few years ago. Right after the... I'm not gonna say 'shooting' — I'm just gonna call it a murder."

"And you never spoke again?"

"Remember what Tony Soprano used to say? 'Dead to

me'. That's my cousin Chris. Dead as a duck in ya mama's gumbo. Y'all want another beer?"

Skip and A.A. glanced at each other. Abasolo said, "You mean another delicious Seven-up? One's my limit."

Skip said, "Yeah, we better go. Listen, can't thank you enough for this."

"You know something?" Abasolo said. "You two look kind of alike."

"Me and Langdon? How you get that?"

"You and Fazzio."

"What?" Clarke looked taken aback. "The hell we do. Nobody's ever said that before."

"The shaved head's new, right? I think it's that."

"Aw shit. Whoever told white people they could shave their heads? That's supposed to be a black thing."

Skip couldn't resist. "Goddamn cultural appropriation," she said.

18

C ody was feeling more and more confident about her disguise, particularly when she wore the white shirt and tie. Once a girl actually gave her her phone number.

"Had to be a lesbian," Mikey said.

When an older man did the same thing, even Mikey was impressed. But the best thing of all was the day she fooled the cop. She was walking the dogs in Washington Square Park, and had bent down to pick up some poop when she thought she heard a familiar voice.

Standing up, she saw Skip not fifteen feet away, in jeans and an Ole Miss sweatshirt, with a bearlike man even bigger than she was, and the cutest little spaniel in the world — her good friend, Rambla! Seeing Rambla, Andy J. strained at his leash.

"Is your dog a boy?" the cop called out. "I'm afraid she encourages them."

Cody didn't dare speak. She was so afraid Rambla would greet her! But evidently they were far enough apart that the dog couldn't recognize her. She gave a weak smile and turned away, walking in the opposite direction as quickly as she could, expecting heavy footsteps behind her as realization dawned. But all was quiet — that is, at least until Marcia and Dr. John got into a squabble about... well, what was it about? Cody asked, but they wouldn't say. Inappropriate sniffing, she thought.

She was almost home when the footsteps finally came. She knew the last thing she should do was let the cop see her face or hear her voice, so she started to walk so fast the dogs' feet had to move like little eggbeaters to keep up. She hated doing it to them, she really did, but then again, they wouldn't have appreciated being detained in a shelter while she was at City Prison.

Panicked, she tried to come up with a plan. How do you run with four tiny dogs that have legs the length of forks?

Impossible, so how do you hide?

She decided the best plan was to stay in a crowd, and looked around for one. Yes! Across the street was a gaggle of girls, one of them wearing a tiara and veil. In less than a week, Cody had learned to recognize a bachelorette party when she saw one. This one would be perfect.

Quickly, she crossed to the other side, developing a plan along the way. She slipped into the very middle of the pack, transferring all the leashes to one hand and tipping her fedora in a ringmaster's exaggerated gesture. "Hello, beautiful ladies, and welcome to New Orleans."

She'd thought to go on a bit about their beauty and the virtues of their choice of venue, but there was no need. All fifteen of them immediately fell upon the dogs, cuddling, cooing, and petting, pretty much leaving the cute faux-boy in their midst to his own devices. Cody managed to maneuver back towards the street, and saw no cop in sight. Like Cody, Skip would be hampered by her canine companion and all the more visible for her large male human one. But Cody saw nothing except the backs of tourists and a well-dressed guy in dreads, another in a tux — a musician and a waiter, probably.

So… was she really being followed or was it her imagination? She had just time to decide that it was only paranoia before being drawn into a swamp of doggie questions. What were their names? Did they make good pets? Wasn't it hard to groom them, with all that fur? And then someone noticed she was a cute boy. "Hey, you want to meet us later? We're going to House of Blues."

She couldn't wait to tell Mikey what a good boy she was.

She got to tell Mikey and Elliott at the same time. They were both in the courtyard when she returned, having pink cocktails. Elliott jumped up. "Well, if it isn't Mr. C.T. Thibodeaux! Let me look at you, C.T."

Cody unleashed the dogs and did a "Ta-Da" thing, once again tipping the fedora and holding it aloft.

"You make a downright adorable boy! Come here and give me a hug." Cody did, gladly. That warmed her heart. "And please beware of dirty old men. I can't tell if you're worse jailbait as a boy or a girl."

"I'm going to take that as a compliment," she said, and smiled as best she could.

But her expression must have somehow betrayed her. Despite her best effort to keep it light, Elliott still practically jumped a foot — "What'd I say?"

He had no idea, of course, that she'd been hooking for Miguel for two years, and she had no intention of telling him. But she couldn't help it. Well-intentioned as she knew it was, the jailbait remark had hurt a little.

"Oh, it's not you! That just reminded me of something that happened today." She was struggling to manufacture a plausible story when she was interrupted by a loud, insistent knocking on the front gate, followed by a symphony of shrill, persistent barking.

"Cheese it, the cops." Mikey said.

Elliott stared at him. "Whatever that means, you aren't kidding," said Elliott. "That sure sounded like a police knock. What do we do with C.T. here?"

"How about we just don't let 'em in?" Cody suggested.

"Sounds like a plan," Mikey left to negotiate, followed by four bundles of extremely vocal fur, outraged and hopping up and down.

They could hear him saying things like, "Who's there? Can I help you?"

Finally, he came back. "Not the cops. I dunno. Just some French Quarter crazy, I guess. Nobody was there. I opened the door and there were a few people walking down the street, but none of them turned around."

"What kind of people?" asked Cody.

"Just regular people. Tourist couple. Guy with dreads. That artist who wears the top hat. Nobody who looked likely."

"THIS ONE'S as clean as Cody's," said Skip. She and Abasolo were going over the crime scene reports on the double murder at Emily Martinez's house.

"Cody's still our best bet," Abasolo answered. "Let's go. We don't want to keep the captain waiting."

They'd taken the unusual step of asking her to meet them outside headquarters, in fact clear outside the neighborhood, at the CC's coffeehouse on Esplanade. She wasn't happy.

"What's this all about?" she snapped, scowling.

Skip glanced at Abasolo, silently pleading with him to exercise his famous charm and get the meeting on track. He grinned. "Commander, you know we wouldn't have done this if it weren't important. We've really got a situation."

"What you've got is a double murder to solve. And maybe a serial killer to catch."

"Let me show you something." Skip handed over her phone, set to show the picture Cody had sent. "Recognize this guy?"

"Sure, It's Fazzio. He's still wearing those stupid shades. Says he got them for his birthday. Or something."

"Remember Cody Thibodeaux, the pink-haired girl we interviewed? The one who got away from that Magazine St. scene?"

Seeing the commander nod, she continued. "Cody bolted in the middle of the interview, and later sent this picture to Melody at Covenant House. See the text message with it? 'This is the whale'."

Another nod.

"That's what she calls the guy who attacked her."

Finally getting it, Cappello rose halfway out of her chair — or so it seemed to Skip. She could have sworn the commander's hair stood up at least another inch on top of her head. "Are you kidding me? You're telling me this freak is one of our guys? A Homicide cop?"

Once again, Abasolo gave the commander his killer grin. "See? Aren't you glad we didn't talk about this in the office?"

She shut him down with a stare that could have burned a hole in his Kevlar vest.

"Fazzio looks like a lot of people. He's famous for being a Jim Forbes look-alike."

"We checked on Forbes," A.A. reported. "He was in Mexico the night of the first murder."

Skip took over: "We've talked to a couple of Chris's friends and colleagues. Without telling them anything, of course." She added the last part when she saw the look on Cappello's face. "What they said was pretty scary."

She and Abasolo told the two stories between them—Duckworth's negative assessment; Clarke's regretful understanding.

"And?" said Cappello when they'd laid it out. "What do you want to do next? Search his house? What's your probable cause? That some of his colleagues don't like him?"

"With all due respect, Commander, we have a witness who's identified him as her attacker."

"See, that's the problem," the commander said. "You don't have that witness."

Skip sipped her skinny vanilla latte like an automaton, for once not even tasting it. "We had to tell you sometime, right? We thought this was the right time — after we'd done enough work to see if there was anything there. And what we found we couldn't ignore. Do you think we're right about that?"

The commander sat back and thought about it.

Abasolo gave Skip a tiny nod to show he approved.

Finally Cappello said, "You're right. I'm sorry I got upset." Long pause. "But Jesus Christ motherfucker goddammit!"

Unwittingly, Skip laughed. Which had the effect of letting Cappello hear herself. Next thing you know they were all laughing.

Abasolo broke the moment. "Don't ask me what was funny, but I think I feel better."

"What we need," Skip said, "is a direction. The last thing

we want to do is tip off Fazz... umm... let's just call him the whale. We want to avoid giving him a chance to guess he's a suspect, so we're sure not going to question him or any more of his friends. Given that, where do we look for evidence?"

"How about the eye injury?"

"Good idea! No way we can get his medical records, even if we could find out who his doctor is. Any way you can get him to take off his glasses?" Skip paused. "I mean, you're his boss. Can you say he has to look you in the eye or something?"

"All that would tell us is that he does have an injury. We need the thing she stabbed him with."

"Yeah, We thought of that too. But she got away too quick to ask her."

Cappello looked hopeful, as if she'd had a thought. "Anything from the double murder? A teensy-tiny little hair or fingerprint? Something?"

"So far nada."

Cappello rose again, this time all the way. "Okay, then. You've got to find the missing witness. There's really no way around it." And she left them to pay the bill.

"Tell us something we don't know," Abasolo said.

"It doesn't matter," Skip said. "Mission accomplished."

"How's that?"

"We can't blindside her any more, right? We've already done that. So now we can go ahead and solve the case with her blessing."

"No question," he said, "that you are a glass half full kind of person."

19

"Guy with dreads?" asked Cody. "Could he have been the one knocking? What was he wearing?"

"He could have been, sure. But so could several people. He was wearing very clean, perfectly faded jeans and a leather jacket," Mikey said. "Nice clothes, like he was sort of a dandy." He paused, seeing her reaction. "What? I don't like that look on your face. You know him?"

"I think so, yeah. And I saw him a while ago — from the back. I thought he was following me, but he went on past. He must have doubled back."

Elliott moaned. "This is not good. Very un-good."

"No, it's okay. He's probably just my friend Terry's boyfriend. The handsy one, remember?"

"Like I mentioned," Elliott said, "not good. But at least he's not a serial killer."

"That we know of," Mikey added.

"This is nothing I can't handle," Cody said, and wondered why Elliott looked so troubled.

She stared at him until he said, "You're too young for all this, you know that? Whatever you're running from, think maybe you've run long enough? Maybe we just need to bring the cops in on it?"

She'd gotten past the point of crying every time someone said something nice to her, but this got to her. Her eyes clouded up. "Elliott, you're so sweet! But not yet, ok? For now, I'm good. Hey, I almost forgot — got a present for you." She ducked into the slave quarters to get it.

When she came back, he and Mikey were engaged in animated conversation.

" 'Cheese it! The cops?' " Elliott was saying sarcastically. "Whatthehell is that?"

Cody'd been wondering the same thing.

"It means 'Flee! All is discovered.' Or something like that. You never heard it before?"

Both Mikey and Cody shook their heads.

"Sigh. I'm surrounded by ignoramuses. Did neither of you ever see The Bowery Boys?"

"What's that?" they asked in unison.

"You know — those really, really old movies with a guy in a weird hat? Sort of a street gang that was always getting in trouble. But funny." Seeing their blank expressions, he abandoned the effort. "Oh, never mind, it was just something they said in old movies." He picked up his phone to search. "Here it is — 'Cheese it, the cops' —ok, maybe it meant something more like stop than flee. But seems to me they always ran out the back door when anyone said it."

"I like it," said Cody, suddenly feeling shy. She could see Mikey was gearing up for another onslaught of good-natured peer abuse, but she wanted to change the subject. "Elliott, I did a portrait for you."

He took the drawing and fussed over it as if it were the finest work of a Grand Master, once again warming her heart so much she knew it would have made her cry a few days ago. But it didn't now. It made her smile. She was starting to get used to her new life. Actually, to life.

Because the way she'd been living wasn't living at all. It was just trying to get through without feeling the hurt and humiliation and, often, the pain. The fear was almost the worst — when you knew you could be raped or beaten every day, you never had a moment of real life, life in which you didn't have to be either hurt or afraid of being hurt.

Every second of every day she counted her newfound blessings and became more desperate to keep them. Bad enough the whale was still out there, but now she sensed a threat on a whole other level. She had to fix it somehow. She was free now, and she could fix it. She just had to figure out how.

When Elliott had left and Mikey had gone to work, she sat down to think about what had just happened with Winston. Because the guy in the dreads had to be Winston. What would have happened, she wondered, if she'd answered the door herself? Well, no problem, she'd never do that. Whatever he was up to, it couldn't be good. If Terry hadn't killed Miguel, she was pretty sure Winston probably had — and would probably kill her just as handily. Somebody in that house had written the address of the Bayou Motel on a card for a gym and underlined it twice. And neither of them had any reason to go there — unless it involved Miguel.

She needed a plan.

She thought a long while, the outline of one forming in her mind. She knew what she needed to happen, but it was more like a pipe dream than a game plan. She had no idea how to get anyone to do what she wanted — and there were plenty of other actors in the movie in her head.

She tried to think like a cop. Just about everybody

involved in this thing was a cop. Skip and Abasolo hadn't arrested the whale on the strength of the picture she'd sent Melody. She knew because she was checking local stations and sites obsessively. What else did they need? she wondered. What could she do to make it happen?

She kept turning it over and over in her mind, and the next day, as she sat on the Decatur St. sidewalk— drawing a portrait of a customer who wouldn't stay off his damn cell phone long enough to give her time to see what he looked like — an idea hit her.

She might have something she could use as leverage — something the whale would pay a lot for.

THE SEARCH for Cody took Skip back in time — to a similar search, long ago, for a young Melody. The irony of having to go to Melody as the city's leading expert on runaways wasn't lost on her.

The current scene wasn't all that different, either. Runaways stuck together, they came out at night, they congregated in the French Quarter, the Marigny, the Bywater — in parks, by the river, begging on Decatur Street — and the girls still danced in sleazy clubs. Given Cody's history, Skip hoped she'd recognize the danger in that, but she knew she couldn't count on it. People gravitated to what they knew. She decided to start on Bourbon Street while Abasolo hit the parks, each armed with the picture Stella had drawn of Cody.

As she stood in the half-light of a club whose owners had had the chutzpah to name Jailbait, she pondered the hopelessness of anyone in a place like this ever telling a cop anything besides their names. Her stomach flipped, thinking of Cody in that place. After a few half-hearted inquiries, she decided to come back later for the night shift.

She took to stopping everyone on the street who might be under twenty, even if they looked like a tourist. With that pink hair, Cody was pretty distinctive — anyone at all might have noticed her. And indeed a couple of people thought they might have, they just weren't sure where.

She was about to try Daddy's Girls, the most notorious club of all, when her phone signaled a text. Thinking it might be Abasolo, she grabbed for it.

It was from Cody, using a new phone. Skip had tried the old one a hundred times, but the kid had done what you do with a burner phone, she surmised— burned it before it burned her.

"Be at Lafitte In Exile at 5 p.m. today," it read. "The whale will be out front. I'll be the one in the cute hat. Stay out of sight till you see us together."

She texted back frantically. "Cody, no! Too dangerous. Meet me now and we'll figure something out."

After twenty minutes, she knew she wasn't going to hear back. She called Abasolo. "Thank God," he said. "I'm at Woldenberg Park and I'm getting depressed. Bunch of young white drunks with buzz cuts and enough ink on 'em to print a newspaper. I think I like the gutterpunks better. These guys look like skinheads with hair. Although not much hair."

"Stay where you are, I'm coming over."

"Good. These dudes are scaring me."

"I heard from her." She told him what was going on. They had an hour to figure out a strategy.

There were three good vantage points: Inside the bar itself; in the Clover Grill on the other side of Bourbon Street; and inside The Washing Well across Dumaine Street.

Since Lafitte In Exile was a gay bar, Abasolo, despite his sober status, was the obvious designated barfly. And Skip deemed the Washing Well a better vantage point than the Clover Grill, since Dumaine St. was narrower than Bourbon, with less traffic. Naturally, they arrived not at five, but a good deal before.

Skip was a long-time a customer at The Washing Well, having lived only a few blocks away for years. She was still in the neighborhood every day — to drop Rambla off — so she'd seen no reason to switch loyalties. Personnel hardly ever changed there. For the last few years, Margo, a young African-American woman, had reigned over the laundry. And it really was a reign — because very likely no other business in the French Quarter had so many neighborhood regulars. That meant Margo knew everyone and also knew everything about them. She was discreet about business secrets, like lipstick on gentlemen's apparel, but other than that, she was absolutely the best source of local news who didn't work for a TV station. Very local indeed — her friends called her "the eyes and ears of the French Quarter." She could tell you who was planning to move Uptown, who'd moved in with their mama to take advantage of Airbnb, who'd moved out on their husband, and who was so sick they couldn't move a muscle.

She frowned when she saw Skip. "Hey, Skip, you picking something up? I don't remember... oh, wait... you here for Sheila's red cocktail dress?"

Skip had to smile. She didn't pick up the Ritter-Scoggin laundry any more, but it was sweet of Margo to remember. "Actually here on business," she said.

"Uh-oh. What'd we do?"

"I need to ask a big favor. Can I park myself over there and look out that window for a few minutes?"

Margo looked outraged. "You telling me a crime's about to go down out there?"

"Not that I know of. But I did get a tip somebody's going to be there that I need to talk to. Hey, actually... you might have seen her." She pulled out Cody's picture and showed it. "Ring a bell?"

"Not even close."

"She doesn't look dangerous, does she?"

Finally Margo smiled — "If you can get those shutters open, you're welcome to it. I think the last time anybody tried was before I came to work here."

As it happened, probably no one had bothered, because they opened easily. Skip looked at her watch and texted Abasolo: "Four-forty-five and all's well."

He answered, "Here too. Aside from the beer-and-smoke aroma."

They both settled in to wait, hoping the after-work crowd on the sidewalk didn't thicken too fast. So far it was pretty quiet. Ten minutes later, at almost exactly four-fifty-five, Fazzio showed up.

Skip's breath caught. Until then, she hadn't really believed it would happen. She couldn't risk texting, couldn't take her eyes off him, but she had A.A. on speed dial. "He's out there," she said. "See him?"

"Roger. But no Cody yet."

"Standing by."

She didn't have to stand long, although it wasn't Cody's appearance that got her attention. The first thing she saw was Fazzio's mouth moving, apparently shouting something, his face scrunched in agitation. But she couldn't see who he was shouting at. Then she saw him take off running across Bourbon Street. Another nanosecond and Abasolo was after him like a bullet. But from her side window, she could see only Lafitte In Exile, not the other side of Bourbon Street.

She hurtled around the counter and out the door, jostling Margo in the process. "Excuse me!" she heard herself shout, and plowed into a customer who hadn't seen her coming.

"Whathehell you think you're doing?" the man yelled, grabbing at Skip's arm, which she jerked away, pulling her gun from her shoulder holster.

"Hey, no need for that. I didn't mean anything," she heard him say, but reassuring him was the farthest thing from her mind. Despite her assurance to Margo, there was evidently a crime in progress.

Fazzio and Abasolo were closing in on what looked like a man kidnapping a young boy. Whoever they were, it wasn't father and son. The man was in his 30s, black and wearing dreads, and the boy was a teen-ager, no older than fourteen probably, white and wearing a hat. The man spun the boy around to face the two cops, his hand at the kid's back, maybe holding a gun or knife, the boy kicking, struggling so hard his hat fell off.

The kid had surprisingly feminine features, Skip noticed, and suddenly remembered something: "I'll be the one in the cute hat!"

She shouted, "Let her go or I'll blow your head off!"

The man looked at her and for a moment seemed to be processing the fact that a tall white woman in ordinary clothes had a gun trained on him. As soon as it registered, he pushed the kid to the sidewalk and took off on Dumaine towards the river.

He was fast. Fazzio shot past Skip and the kid, and then Abasolo did, swearing. That was good with Skip. She had on her badass boots, ideal for thug-chasing, but for now she was content to babysit — especially since the baby was the most important witness in the ugliest case she'd seen in a long time. And desperately needed her help.

She knelt down. "Cody, you okay?"

"Omigod! Skip." The girl held up her right hand, which she'd evidently stuck out to break her fall. It didn't look right. Skip thought it was probably broken, but that didn't stop Cody from putting both arms around Skip's neck. "That was him! The guy who handcuffed me. You've gotta go after him." She was screaming, frantic.

"The black guy?"

"No, the other one." Sobbing now. "The cop."

Skip gently dislodged herself from the hug, so she could see the kid's face. "So who just tried to kidnap you?"

"That was the guy who killed Miguel."

Whathehell? Trying to process what her brain couldn't take in, Skip felt like the would-be kidnapper who couldn't get over who was busting him just then. She hadn't gotten very far when she heard shots — three of them, in quick succession.

20

I t took every ounce of her will power not to take off down the street before calling for back-up and packing Cody off to temporary sanctuary at the Washing Well, with the admonition that she was dead meat if she moved a muscle till Skip got back.

"And I mean that," she finished. "You want to end up in child protection?" This wasn't kosher, but her partner might be down and so long as no one knew where the kid was she'd be safe.

The look on Cody's face said, "Message received," but Skip barely saw it. Her phone had just registered a text from Abasolo: "All ok. Suspect shot."

"Dead?" she texted back.

"Negative. Shoulder."

She went ahead and gave him a call. "Back-up's on the way. You need me?"

"No, we're good. The guy with dreads shot at us twice, though. Just turned around and fired in mid-stride, like some cowboy in a Western. Fortunately no one was hurt.

Take care of that kid, whoever he is. Hey, did Cody ever show?"

"That was Cody — 'the one in the cute hat', remember?"

"Seriously? I'm starting to think young Miss Cordelia's something to be reckoned with. I don't know what she did just now, but I think it might have flushed out some answers."

He was being circumspect, she knew. He didn't want to say, "flushed out a serial killer" in front of the serial killer himself.

"Speaking of that," she said, "which one of you shot the perp?"

"Oh, Fazzio. Happy to say."

Happy because any shooting is controversial, she imagined. But happier because it meant Fazzio would be tied up with department red tape while they made their case against him.

She hung up and turned to Cody. "How's that arm?"

"I'm okay. Did anyone get shot?"

"The guy who tried to kidnap you got shot in the shoulder."

"Winston?"

"Oh, you know him. Okay, more on that later. Let's get you to the hospital." Not bothering with an ambulance, Skip arranged for transportation for Abasolo, piled Cody into her district car, and turned on the siren.

As they waited to get checked in, Skip said, "Do you want to call your grandmother or do you want me to?"

Cody looked stricken, as if she hadn't really thought about what came next. She took a moment to reply, clearly thinking it through. "Can we wait until... umm... until, you know, you get the whale?"

There was something whiny about the way she said it,

something Skip translated as urgent. Suddenly a few pennies at once dropped. "Are you afraid he's going to go after your grandmother? Is that why you've been leading us such a merry chase?"

Cody nodded, not speaking, letting her face say it all.

"Ohhhh. Okay. That explains a lot. Well, listen, baby — the tabby's exited the suitcase..."

Seeing the girl's confused look, she stopped herself. "Sorry. I've started talking like my learned partner. I meant the secret's out — he knows where you are. So he has no motive to go torture your grandma to tell him."

Cody winced at the word "torture", but she nodded, an array of emotions flitting across her face as she took it in. "Let me call her," she said.

She stepped outside to do it, per hospital rules, with Skip watching at a discreet distance. She saw a look of pure childlike joy replace the worry, and then Cody looked up at her, face shining like a kid at Christmas. "She's coming. What hospital's this?"

WHILE SHE WAITED to get her wrist X-rayed and get otherwise checked out, Cody reflected that, aside from nearly getting kidnapped and Winston getting shot, things had worked out a lot better than she had any right to hope. Winston was out of commission, the cops were taking her seriously about the whale, and Langdon was right — cats were out of bags.

She texted Mikey: Can someone else feed the dogs? Did something dumb. Broken hand, but everything's good! With cops now, Maw-Maw coming. Keep the note! But you can read it. C. T.

The point of the note she'd left him was to back up her story — that she wasn't a blackmailer, but a concerned citizen setting a tiny trap for a couple of dangerous criminals. Right, she thought now. I'm definitely going down.

It seemed like a pretty lame explanation.

But the thing was that during her two years in Houston, there wasn't a lot to do when she wasn't working except watch TV. There was a contingent in the house that liked Disney movies, but most of the girls went in for cop shows, and Cody was a big fan. She knew exactly how to set a trap — you threatened and then you blackmailed. And sometimes you dangled bait. She did both.

First, she'd called the police and asked for Homicide, just like a regular citizen. "I've got a tip for the bald guy," she said.

The guy who answered said in a bored tone, "Who is this? Best I can do is take a message for him."

"I don't know his name."

"Just give me yours."

She reached back in her memory. The whale had called her a name and she wasn't likely to forget it. "Monica," she said.

"Okay, what's the message?"

"I'm the only one who can give it to him."

"Look, we got bald guys coming out the ass around here."

"This one's white. With a shaved head." She paused for effect. "And shades. He has an eye injury."

"Oh... that's why he's wearing the damn shades."

The phone made mechanical sounds and then she got a voice message, "This is Chris Fazzio. Leave a message."

"This is Monica," she said. "From Magazine St. You remember me... I was the one in the T-shirt with the kitty on it. I have something of yours. It's DNA. I can prove you're the guy, but it doesn't have to go that way. I like you; I want to give you a way out. Meet me in front of Lafitte In Exile at 5 o'clock tomorrow — and bring $100,000. In a backpack."

She'd picked an arbitrary amount, figuring he definitely wasn't going to bring any money — he was just going to try to kill her. The question was would he show up at all? Cops must get a lot of crank calls. But she thought the shirt and the name ought to convince him she was real.

And now for the tricky part. She called Winston. "Hey. It's Cody."

"You little bitch, I'm gonna..."

"I know you killed Miguel."

"What the fuck...?"

"Why else are stalking me? You want to kill me or warn me off or... you know... like I said, kill me... but it doesn't have to go that way." She was liking that phrase. "I could just go right to the police. Now. Before you can get to me."

"I'm outside your house right now. The crib with the dogs."

"Well, I'm right by the police station. All I have to do is walk in the door. But I'm not going to. I'm leaving now. I'll be outside Lafitte In Exile at 5 o'clock this afternoon. Bring me $20,000 and you'll never see me again."

"Really?" He sounded pretty sarcastic. "You'd just go away for twenty thousand dollars?"

"You know what I've been through, dude. I need to get out of here. Just give me the seed money, and I'm gone."

"You really think I've got twenty thousand dollars lying around?"

"I'll take ten."

"I can get you a thousand."

"Ha! That won't get me as far as Memphis."

"Be there or be square." He hung up.

Cody was shaking. She shook throughout the phone call, partly out of nervousness, but now at the realization she'd actually pulled this thing off. The first part of it, anyway. He'd agreed to meet her. Hadn't he? She was pretty damn sure that was what he meant.

Now to get Skip on board.

Exactly what was going to happen at five o'clock she wasn't sure, but all she needed was for Winston and the whale to show up. If only one of them did, she was still ahead. She couldn't go on the way she had— afraid for her own life and Maw-Maw's at Winston's hands or the whale's. She had to do something.

What she was hoping for was something like this: They'd both be on the sidewalk in front of the bar, she'd walk over from the Clover Grill, and then Langdon would pop by and sort it all out.

She'd recorded both the calls. So they'd at least have to explain their presence. And the cops would have to listen to her. She was their only witness in a huge case.

But the whole thing fell apart when Winston turned up early, decided to wait for her in the Clover Grill, and tried to kidnap her.

He had a gun too. Cody shivered. There was no question in her mind he planned to kill her.

21

Once again Steve brought Rambla into the office, Skip's condition for interviewing the kid that night instead of heeding her doctors' plea for rest.

"I want you to get her while she's still raw," the commander had said, and Skip knew it had to be done, even though Cody had a couple of broken metacarpals and a prescription for painkillers.

Cody was on the commander's side. "I just want to get it done," she said. "I'm not taking anything till I've talked to you." They let her ride from the hospital to headquarters with her granny, Chantelle Thibodeaux, and Chantelle's improbably handsome boy friend. The reunion was something to see, with tears on both sides and Cody collapsing against the woman she called "Maw-Maw" pretty much like an empty suit of clothes. It just seemed like the energy drained out of her until Chantelle managed to release enough Maw-Maw love to pump her up again. When Cody came up for air, she had color in her cheeks.

Abasolo said, "Hey, you look okay. I think you might make it."

"She's gonna make it," Chantelle said grimly, an angry glint in her eye. Although Skip didn't think Abasolo was the object of her anger. She also thought she wouldn't want to get on the wrong side of Chantelle.

"There's no doubt in my mind, Mrs. Thibodeaux," Abasolo said. "I can honestly say this is the toughest kid I've ever seen." The lovefest might have gone on for a while except that it was interrupted by two skinny young guys, one pretty well inked-up, the other with hair the color of a stop sign, worn in the style of Woody Woodpecker.

"I don't believe what I'm seeing," Cody cried, and the two glued themselves to her the best they could do, considering there was only one of her to go around. "These are my two best friends," she explained. "Elliott and Mikey." Here, she got a little teary. "They've been taking care of me."

"She lies to us," the tatted one said, "but we love her, anyway. We're calling her C.T. these days. Mind telling us who she is?"

"That is me," Cody insisted.

"Cordelia," said Chantelle. "Or Cody."

"And you would be... the famous Maw-Maw?"

"What are you guys doing here?" Cody demanded.

"We read the letter, like you said. And then there's... you know, the news."

"What?" Skip said.

"Oh, don't worry, all it said was an unidentified juvenile. But reading between the lines, we figured Cody could use some back-up." He turned to Maw-Maw and Zachary. "We didn't know y'all would be here."

"Would have been here days ago," Zachary said, "if she..."

Mikey waved a dismissive hand. "Yeah, we know what she's like." To Skip and A.A. he said, "We did tell her to call you guys. Just for the record." He turned back to Cody and her family. "Y'all need a place to stay tonight? I could bunk at my folks'."

Finally the two cops got her disentangled from her suddenly bountiful family and into headquarters, where she was nearly killed with kisses by Rambla.

After quick introductions, Steve left, Zachary left, and the BFF's left. Only Chantelle and Rambla stayed for the interview.

Tough as she was, Cody clearly had trouble telling her story, and she was clearly in pain. Finally, A.A. could stand it no longer. "Won't you at least take some aspirin?"

She shook her head. "I want to get this out. And then I want a hamburger and fries. But not from the Clover Grill."

The teetering logistics of the thing made Skip shiver. How was it even possible for a 16-year-old to think she could pull off something like that? But she reflected that most of "what's-the-worst-that-can-happen?" had already happened to this kid. If she hadn't developed resourcefulness, she'd probably be dead.

The thing she was confused about was why Cody thought Winston had killed Miguel Bustamente. "I'm not sure he did," she said. "I think Terry might have."

"So why did Winston keep trying to kill you?"

She doubled up on her dog-patting speed. "I don't think Terry knew he was doing it. But maybe I just want to think that."

"Still, why would he do it?"

"Oh, to protect her. She probably told him I accused her of it to her face... I mean, I was kind of congratulating her, but..."

"Cody," interjected Chantelle.

The girl answered her grandmother in such a sincere and matter-of-fact way it almost made Skip smile. "Maw-Maw, I'm not sorry I said it — somebody needed to kill him." Cody turned back to the cops. "Winston needs Terry. She brings him money and keeps a nice home for him and... she's just a good person."

Skip thought, There's gotta be more to it than that. But she left it for now. She had to admit either one of the two would make a pretty decent suspect. Especially since it was obvious Winston would have killed Cody to keep her quiet.

"Okay," she said, "about the whale." She phrased her next sentence carefully. "Did you see him today?"

"You mean was that him in front of Lafitte In Exile? The guy who chased Winston?"

And shot him, Skip thought. She nodded.

"I think so."

"Think hard, Cody. Are you sure?"

The girl closed her eyes and squinched them up. She opened them. "Pretty sure."

Skip pointedly didn't look at Abasolo, tried to show no emotion as her hopes for a search warrant slid precariously out of sight. "He's the guy you sent the picture of, right?"

"Yes. But I'd feel better if I could see him without the shades."

"I think we could do that. But he's with Winston now. How about this — could you play us that recording again? The one you made of your message for him?"

This was the part that caught her attention: I have something of yours. It's DNA. I can prove you're the guy, but it doesn't have to go that way. I like you; I want to give you a way out. Meet me in front of Lafitte In Exile at 5 o'clock tomorrow — and bring $100,000. In a backpack.

"We checked his backpack," she said. "It just had a couple of books and a flashlight in it."

"Does that matter?" Cody asked. "The idea was to get him to... you know, try to kill me." The matter-of-fact way she said it broke Skip's heart. "I mean, why should he just give me money when he could kill me? He's bigger and he's got a gun. He came, didn't he? So it worked." By the end of the speech she was sounding downright defiant.

Abasolo said, "That's cold logic for you, " which allowed Skip to sneak her question while Cody pondered whether or not he was being ironic.

"What were you threatening him with? What DNA do you have?"

"Oh. Well. I don't have it any more. But he wouldn't know that." She pulled a sharp-looking hairpin from a pocket. "At Miguel's we all had to wear these whenever we had a trick. You can hide them, no problem, if you actually have hair..." she ran a rueful hand through her boy-buzz. "If you have a problem, you go like this..." She repeated the action with two hands, seductively, "and he thinks it's a come-on, but you take the pin out when you do it and then, before he sees it coming, you jab it in his eye.

"I don't know if I got his actual eye, but I sure drew blood. So... DNA." She shook her head, staring at the pin. "But I washed it. Actually, I put it in a pan of water and boiled it." She stole a look at her grandmother. "I'm sorry, Maw-Maw. I did it at St. Anthony's. I had to. I couldn't throw it away."

"Of course you couldn't, baby. That little thing saved your life."

Skip extracted a plastic bag from her pocket and held it out for the pin. "Well, let's test it anyhow. Maybe there's a trace."

Cody hesitated.

"Don't worry, we'll return it."

She dropped it in the bag.

Abasolo sighed. "Why couldn't he have just left his phone at the scene or something?"

"Sure would have been convenient," Chantelle said.

Skip was staring at Cody. She'd covered her face with both hands, but before she managed, Skip got a glimpse of it — it was a mask of horror. Rambla whined, protesting the absence of the kid's compulsive petting.

Chantelle rested a gentle hand on Cody's shoulder blades. "What is it, baby?"

Cody dropped her hands, looking up at them like someone had died. "I screwed up," she whispered. "I screwed up big-time."

22

C ody was mortified. She could barely get the words out, and when they came, they were barely a whisper. "He did leave his phone."

She stared at the cops, who remained impassive, waiting for more. Maw-Maw was beside her, a hand on her shoulder. She gave Cody a sympathetic squeeze. Finally Skip said, "Did you take it with you?"

Cody nodded. "I think so. Yes! I know I did. I used it to call Uber. I went to that place on Canal Street. Where I left the gym bag."

Skip nodded. "Yes. The Palace Café. Did you put it in the gym bag?"

"I'm trying to remember... so much happened that night..."

"Well, we didn't find it there," Abasolo said. "I wonder if you put it somewhere out of habit. A pocket, maybe? Where do you normally keep your phone?"

Cody bowed her head, tongue-tied. His question made her think of her former life and that made her feel ashamed. Once more she understood how different her life was from that of the average teen-ager. She didn't feel like clueing him in. Instead, she just shrugged. She couldn't remember something so tiny, so trivial as whether she'd put a phone in her pocket or her... well, where else was there? She didn't have a purse. She sure couldn't remember putting it in the gym bag, although maybe she had.

"Did you call anybody?"

"I don't think so."

"Well, let's see if we can go back in time. You put something in the gym bag, right? That night shirt, for instance—did you put that there?"

"Wait!" Cody could see herself, terrified, trying to think, trying to escape, grabbing anything she thought she might need. "First I put my clothes in the bag. I just stuffed things in it and then found that back porch thing and slid down the pole. And then I opened the bag and dressed. I remember something now... I took out the phone and the money. But the phone dropped down in the bag and..." she caught her breath, remembering. "I cut myself trying to find it. And then I used it for Uber and never thought about it again. See..." she thought she could say it now... "we weren't allowed.. I mean, I didn't miss it because I'd never had a phone before. I must have put it down and forgotten about it."

That night was such a blur. Where could she have put it down?

"Bathroom?" Skip said. "That's usually where I lose things."

Cody could see herself dressing in that little entryway, practically on the street. It had been so cold. She saw herself hugging her hoodie around her. "Oh. My. God."

Abasolo patted her back. "Are you remembering something?"

Cody pointed at her fleece-covered torso. "I boosted this jacket." She stole a glance at Maw-Maw. "I'm sorry, Maw-Maw, I know I wasn't raised that way..."

Maw-Maw rolled her eyes. "Dawlin', Lord knows how you were raised. I'm just glad you had enough sense to get yourself something to keep you warm." Which made Cody smile. It was true. Her drug-addict mama hadn't exactly hauled her out of bed every week and dragged her off to Sunday school.

She looked back at the cops, saw they were nearly jumping out of their skin, waiting for her to finish what she'd started. "When I came out of the bathroom at the Palace, I saw this jacket hanging on a hook; so I just took it and left my hoodie instead."

No sooner were the words out than the two cops swung into motion. They turned her and Maw-Maw over to someone else, with some quick instructions, and got out of there fast. The instructions were these — they could go to a restaurant, but an officer would go with them. They could stay at Mikey's friend Marda's, but the same officer would guard the door. "You!" Abasolo pointed a demanding finger at her. "Do not leave your grandma's sight, understand?"

Skip added, "And both of you stay in."

"What about Zachary?"

"He can stick around to protect his women."

That made Cody laugh. Like Maw-Maw needed protection. This was a woman who'd been hunting with her dad and brothers since she was a kid, and never went anywhere without a gun. She could probably shoot better than either of the cops.

"But, sure, Zachary can go out if you need supplies or anything. Officer Paxton'll be there."

There was one last detail to iron out. Cody addressed

her grandmother, "You guys aren't allergic to dogs, are you? Mikey's got four Pomeranians. Cutest little things you ever saw!"

"Those little fluffy things?" Maw-Maw said.

"Shoot! Those ain't dogs. They ain't even big enough to be rug rats. They're more like big fuzzy bugs."

"Rug bugs!" Cody cried delightedly.

They were allowed to drive with Officer Paxton, who knew a great place for burgers and fries, close behind them. The cop even took the orders and got the food, which they took home to eat. Marcia and the band went crazy.

And so, it must be said, did Zachary. In about a minute and a half — the time it took to get to the courtyard with four yipping, prancing, overjoyed, welcoming dogs, Zachary was on the floor, petting, cuddling, feeding them bits of burger... once again making Cody wonder wistfully what it was like to have a grandfather.

"Look at him," Maw-Maw said. "Think he's a keeper?"

She did. She was so happy to be with Maw-Maw and Zachary, actually to feel safe, home, and cared-for that her eyes kept filming over. She really was going to have to get control of that. But it was such a relief not to feel stalked by two separate murderers, to know that finally someone else could take over the responsibility of keeping her and Maw-Maw safe. She hadn't realized how hard it was keeping it all together on her own.

And now she had two broken fingers, painkillers, and the delicious drowsiness that accompanies a far-too-heavy meal. "Where we gon' put you, baby?" Maw-Maw said. "I'm just not comfortable having you sleep out there in that guest house. I want you near me!"

"I could sleep in the first floor bedroom, Maw-Maw. As

long as I can have the dogs with me." The idea of being separated from the band was like a physical threat.

SKIP AND ABASOLO showed their badges at the reception desk of the Palace Cafe and asked for lost and found, describing an old gray hoodie, probably a woman's small.

Skip took a breath, hardly believing it, as the receptionist pulled it out from a shelf in the desk. "I've got that right here," she said, "and there's a reason for that. The owner swapped it out for a better one that belonged to one of our best customers. We were all pretty furious. Normally you wouldn't think a thief would be back, but I kept it because it did have a phone in the pocket, so that's a decent enticement. If she came for it, the minute she stepped in the door I was calling you guys." She sighed. "Does this mean you got her? Our other customer's going to be pretty happy to hear it."

Skip was holding the hoodie, feeling its pockets but finding them empty. "May we ask where the phone is?"

"I have it right...."

"Wait!" She was aghast at the woman's startled expression. "I'm sorry," she said. "But can I ask you not to touch it?"

"Ummm... sure." The receptionist backed away from her desk and the two cops, looking like she was afraid the building might blow up.

Skip held up a plastic bag. "Can you point it out and I'll just scoop it up?"

Nervously, the woman pointed. Skip scooped, and then they left on a cresting wave of apologies. She hadn't really meant to scare anyone out of their eye make-up.

But Fazzio knew Cody'd figured out that he was the

whale, and he had to know Skip and Abasolo would move on him as fast as they could. That made him as dangerous as a startled snake. Abasolo called Read to meet them back at headquarters.

"You guys have got to be kidding. I'm on a date. How about after dinner?"

"Who'd date you, you ugly thing? Come on in and do what you were meant to do."

"You are so not adorable," she answered.

"Put her on speaker," Skip said. And then, "Permy, I hate him. He's a monster. Can you make it quick?"

"If you swear never to call me that again." She was waiting for them when they got there.

After ten minutes in the crime lab, she returned with a report and a smile. "There were quite a few fingerprints on the phone cover, most of them partial and probably from a couple of different people. But..." she presented her prize triumphantly, "... this just might be what you're looking for." Four prints, one of them just about perfect. "And..." she held up a plastic bag... "I have an eyelash."

"Probably not his," Abasolo said. "But the fingerprints..."

"I beg to differ. Probably is. See, what most people forget is, they handled the phone before they put a cover on it. So when they wipe it, they don't think to take the cover off and wipe the back of it. I found the good prints and the eyelash under the cover." She smiled. "You're welcome."

"Nice work," Skip said. "Let's look at the phone."

"I've got it charging now."

They all went back to the crime lab, and Skip did the honors, clicking first on texts, then on email, but nothing. She tried photos next.

The first photo was of the dog Sheba, but there were plenty of others, depicting way more than they wanted to see of her injuries. Pictures of Cody were there too, showing her cuffed to a chair and looking like a small, terrified animal. But that sequence was blessedly short. The photos were absolutely all there was, except for a few apps.

Skip said, "Almost there. All we have to do is confirm the prints. And then let's go get him."

CODY COULDN'T REMEMBER whether it was day or night, and had no idea where she was. She'd been sleeping so deeply that at first all she registered was that Dr. John wasn't in his accustomed place, burrowed into her shoulder like a teddy bear, the other dogs glued to various other parts of her anatomy, enclosing her in a fur cradle that had been the best part of her life recently.

Next she understood that she was in the main house, not her slave quarters, and that Maw-Maw and Zachary were sleeping upstairs. Her mouth felt strange, and her cheeks. There was something tight there. She tried to touch her face to figure it out, but her right hand wouldn't move. And then she discovered that neither hand would move. Suddenly realizing she was restrained, she knew instantly who else had to be in the room.

She screamed.

But no sound came out. Well, that explained her face — her mouth had been duct taped. Her eyes darted, trying to penetrate the darkness, and she saw the silhouette of his body as he fussed with something — his bag. She knew that bag, only this couldn't be that one. He'd replaced it.

In one menacing move, he brought himself so close to her she could smell garlic on his breath. How ordinary, she thought. He might have had spaghetti for dinner. Or pizza.

Just like a regular person. It was so odd to her, because this was no regular person; she'd been right to nickname him the whale. It could have been The Leviathan, or The Mastodon, or Bigfoot. In her mind, he was so much larger than she was, than anyone was, so much more frightening, and yet here he was breathing pizza fumes on her.

Wait, if he was the whale, then he'd killed the dogs! Her precious Pomeranians.

"Monica," he said, "you're so ugly now. You could be any little... girl without your beautiful hair."

There was a word there that Cody didn't catch, something shameful, she thought, some kind of girl. He encircled her throat with his hands, and squeezed. She struggled, or tried to, but her legs were immobile too. She couldn't move. She kept trying and trying to scream, but nothing came out.

He let go and said, "I might kill you that way. Quick and almost painless. That's if you're nice. If you're not, we'll have to go back to our old friends." He drew a big ugly knife from his gym bag and whisked it across her forearm, producing a tiny dark line, letting her see that it was so sharp the slightest touch could draw blood. "I have lot of these and they can carve a person to pieces. You'll be fun. That old lady upstairs? That's just my job. I'll have to do her first, though. Because she might hear us in here... and we don't want to be interrupted. Do we? Tell you what, I'll bring her down so you can watch."

Frantically, Cody shook her head, making whatever noises she could produce in the back of her throat. He leaned close to her face and whispered, suddenly sounding all soft and teasing, like he thought he was a boy friend playing a game with her. "Where's my phone, baby? Hmmm? What'd you do with my phone?

"You know I need my phone. It's got some nice pictures

of you on it. You know, when you had that pretty pink hair? Why'd you cut it off, baby? You're so ugly now. You know?"

In spite of herself, the whispering, cajoling tone was calming her down a little. She tried to get back into baby-hooker mode, to remember what her former self would have done to get her way, but something in her just wouldn't go there. Anything but biting the nose off this man just didn't seem.... wait, could she bite his nose? He had to pull the tape off if he really wanted her to answer. If she whispered, he'd have to lean close, and her head wasn't restrained. Maybe she could just butt him. But biting would be better. He'd yell and that would give Maw-Maw a warning. Well, it was a start. Face it; it's the best I can do.

With no voice she didn't know how to make it happen, but there was really no choice. She had to. She settled for eye contact, trying to make herself look as pitiful as possible. Pitiful and repentant and eager to do the bidding of The Great Whale. Then she had another idea — she started making humming noises in the back of her throat, and nodding.

"You gonna tell me? Huh?"

She nodded vigorously. Moving her head like that, she thought she caught a motion somewhere else in the room. Could that be possible?

"You gonna scream?"

Of course she was. Vigorous headshake. And now she was sure — someone else was in the room.

But before The Whale could rip off her gag, a great barking and yipping arose from outside, along with gate-opening noises. Startled, the whale turned to see what was going on, opening up Cody's line of sight so that she could see what the motion was. Maw-Maw, barefoot in her nightie, had progressed through the room, gun in one hand, the other hand making the "be quiet!" sign, until she was now at point blank range. Cody braced herself for the noise.

And Maw-Maw blew his brains out.

She barely had time to be happy he'd turned at the last minute, had actually seen he was about to die at the hands of her grandmother, when Maw-Maw fell on her, the room exploded with dogs, and Officer Paxton unnecessarily ordered Maw-Maw to drop her gun. Who even knew where the gun was? Maw-Maw and Cody were all tangled up together, the tape now off, Cody unable to say a word or even cry, just let her grandmother hold her.

What happened next, she wasn't too sure, but it seemed as if Zachary had simultaneously let go of the dogs' leashes and knocked Paxton out of the way trying to get to her and Maw-Maw. He was crying. Big ol' six-foot Zachary was bawling his head off. Maw-Maw didn't let go of Cody, though. Zachary hugged them both from behind. He rested his head on Maw-Maw's shoulder.

"Chantelle! I thought I'd lost you."

"Dawlin', when you gon' figure out who you marryin'? Do I look like the kind of woman who gets killed?"

Weirdly, Officer Paxton laughed. Or perhaps it wasn't so weird. Then another thing happened — more cops swarmed in, including Skip and her partner, the handsome dude.

The next part went so fast it was a blur: "Cody, you okay? Chantelle, you?"

"How the hell did he get in here?"

"Where were the dogs?"

And then, "Jesus Christ, look at that. It's Mr. Goodbar. That's why the goddam prints didn't match!"

23

Skip, Abasolo, and Read had been so sure they were going to be able to make an arrest tonight, that Cody would be safe because they knew where the killer was. They felt gut-punched when they compared the prints and found them nothing like Fazzio's. What now? None of them knew. They'd worked so hard, so efficiently, and now, if the perp wasn't Fazzio...

Skip had a bad feeling, a desperately urgent, really twitchy kind of feeling. "Let's go get her!" she blurted.

She got no argument. Abasolo only said, "Yeah", as they ran to Skip's car and drove full-out with siren blaring to Chartres and Dumaine. On the way, they heard Paxton's emergency broadcast — one shot fired, one man down. "Damn!" Abasolo smacked the ceiling of the car. Skip pressed harder on the gas.

They hardly noticed the dead man when they arrived. Their eyes searched the room for Cody, but she wasn't easy to find. Chantelle and Zachary were huddled with her, dwarfing her, everyone still hugging, trying to grasp the fact they were all alive and all safe.

Skip couldn't honestly say she was surprised when they turned over the body and she saw who the dead man was — not Chris Fazzio, but his cousin Gus Clarke.

In a lot of ways, their stories were parallel, the key factor being they'd both been available as targets for Monica.

They figured out how Clarke got in when they found the rope on the balcony. He'd come over the roofs. "See, he must have been watching," Paxton said. "He must have seen Zachary go out with the dogs. We got this row of connected townhouses, so if he hauled himself up down the block— or from somebody's courtyard— he could just go over the roofs. I didn't hear a goddam thing."

Skip nodded. "I used to live in the Quarter. People do it all the time. Sometimes they run all the way from one end to the next. Really annoying."

"He tied a rope to something up there, let himself down to the balcony, and just went in through the door." They looked at it. It even had a deadbolt. He'd done the trick with a glasscutter and suction cup to cut a section of glass out, then he'd reached through and let himself in. Fortunately, at some point Chantelle had heard something and tiptoed to investigate.

When they went back in, Read had something good for them— a bag of what looked like tiny hairs and another of minuscule fibers with a pair of tweezers in it, as if Clarke had used the tweezers to gather them. "They found these in his pockets."

"Already bagged like that?"

"Yes. Can't wait to find out what they are. Trophies, maybe?"

Skip said, "I get the hair, but who takes trophy threads?"

"What I don't get," Paxton said, "is how he knew she was even here."

Skip and Abasolo looked at each other sheepishly. "God-dammit!" Abasolo blurted, and stomped out.

Paxton looked as if he'd been punched. "What did I say?"

"Don't worry about it. He's just been worried about Cody."

But that wasn't it. They both knew they'd tipped Clarke themselves. Maybe he'd put some kind of trackers on their cars. Or maybe not— all he really had to do was follow them.

What Skip didn't get was all the vitriol on the walls. If The Whale wasn't a white racist, it no longer made sense.

FAZZIO WAS STILL UP when they got to his house, if the lights were any indication. He met them at the door, dressed in sweats and running shoes and drinking a beer. Flashing TV images were visible behind him. At his side was a German shepherd so well-behaved Skip was confused till she noticed he was taking cues from his owner, responding to hand signals. "Meet Bruno," his owner said, and Bruno offered a paw to shake.

But the most arresting thing she noticed was that their host sported the faint green and yellow traces of a recent black eye. He seemed surprised to see them. "What's up, dudes? Excuse me — dude and dudette."

"Can we come in?"

"Something wrong?" They could see he didn't want to, but he let them in and led them to a family room outfitted with ancient red sofas a lot more shabby than chic, a rumpled blue stadium blanket, apparently for Bruno, a recliner, and a large television. Papers and magazines littered the floor, along with a few dirty plates and bowls. Fazzio made a face. "Sorry about the mess," he said, and touched his injured eye. "Kind of... getting divorced. Haven't got the hang of housekeeping yet."

Abasolo said, "Tell me you didn't get that eye in that kind of fight."

Fazzio winced. "A little instability going on there. Should have dumped the bitch a long time ago." But from the looks of things, the bitch had dumped him.

"That explains the shades anyhow."

Again he touched his eye, self-consciously, Skip thought, and gave them a half-smile. "Yeah. Who wants to go around explaining some woofer slugged them?" He waved at the sofas, inviting them to sit. "So. What can I do for you?"

"Got some bad news for you."

He listened stoically, every now and then punctuating their tale with something like "woo," or "Jesus!" as they told him his one-time cousin was not only dead but suspected of being the Magazine Street murderer and a possible serial killer.

But there was something off about him, almost as if the story was having no effect on him. Finally, Skip said, "You don't seem surprised."

He made the "what-can-I-tell-you" sign. "Maybe I'm not, you know? Maybe some things are finally falling into place. We were raised together. You know that, right? That's why you're here?"

They nodded.

"Well, Gus has every reason to hate women. God, his aunt was mean to him! AKA my stepmother, by the way. Monica the big black bitch." He sprinkled the speech with racial slurs that went far beyond "black bitch." And when he spoke, a look of such distaste descended on his features that

Skip felt she could actually feel the hatred radiating from him. "You know what she did once? Locked him outside barefoot in 90 degree weather. Man! He had blisters for days!"

Pennies started dropping. Skip thought to herself, That works. He could have told us his own story as Chris's.

He could have hidden his anger, masqueraded as Mr. Nice Guy, while Chris became a rageful nasty racist, and then one day....

Well, she knew it hadn't happened in one day. "You know that Sheba thing?" Fazzio said. "Christ, it gave me the willies! Reminded me of something Gus did when we were kids."

And there it was. The historical connection.

"You know what else she did? She slept in these ugly t-shirts — like with cute animals on them — only they barely covered her ass. She never wore anything under them, and she'd make breakfast in them, one black cheek hanging out when she flipped the bacon, and if she reached up on a shelf— well, front and center anatomy lesson! Even drove me around the bend, and I don't go in for dark meat. Must have done a hell of a number on that kid's head."

Later that evening, a search warrant of Clarke's house turned up pictures, knives, serial killer websites, reams of noxious writings — but oddly, no trophies. So what was up with the hair and bits of fabric?

After her analysis, Read reported a surprising thing: The hair came from a dog.

"And the fibers?" asked Skip.

"Some kind of blue fleece."

They had recently seen those two items close to each other. "Bruno," Abasolo said.

"And that old blanket. Oh my god, are you thinking what I'm thinking?"

"Yeah. That he didn't collect them from a crime scene— he was going to leave them there. If you just kind of scattered them on the floor... like maybe they came off your clothes..."

They checked the schedule— it was Fazzio's day off, so once again, they headed for his house in Metairie, Read in tow, to collect dog hairs and blue fleece for comparison. Bruno seemed a lot happier to see them than his buddy Chris, who'd just left a pile of beer cans in his family room and was in the process of emptying another.

Skip said, "Listen, we know you were on the outs with Gus — when was the last time you saw him?"

Fazzio shrugged. "I don't know — about two years ago, I guess."

"Were you aware he'd shaved his head?"

"What? Like mine?"

Skip nodded. "He looked a lot like you."

"Yeah. Everyone noticed that when we were kids and got our heads shaved. Guess he must have had a little Italian blood too." He smiled, although whether ironically or not, Skip couldn't tell.

"Another question. Did he know Bruno?"

"Oh, sure. Back when we were close, Bruno and him were best friends. Why?"

"Chris. Mind if we have a look around?"

"What? You want to search my house?" Fire shot out of his eyes. And just as quickly went out. "Oh, what the hell. Knock yourself out. I got nothing to hide."

But he went with them as they methodically picked apart each room, starting with the one they were in, but finding nothing till Abasolo reached under the mattress, almost absent-mindedly. "Hey, there's something here. I think it's... uh-huh." He pulled out a phone.

Fazzio said, "That's not mine! How the hell did that get here?"

"I think," Skip said gently, "he may have been trying to frame you."

"What?"

"You know all those racist things he wrote on the walls? Well... how to say this politely... people say they sound like you." What they said was that he was the worst kind of racist, but she didn't want to antagonize him. By now, all his alibis had checked out, Cody had reconsidered her ID, and Clarke had been found to have a healed eye wound, plus healing bruises and cuts consistent with Cody's Buddha-bashing story. The DNA test on the blood found on the bed wasn't yet complete, but they were ninety-nine per cent sure Clarke had acted alone. So why upset Fazzio? Because, despite his differences with Clarke, the two had once been as close as brothers — and Chris's wife had left him. Two bad shocks in the same month.

Fazzio said, "Actually, they sounded more like him."

"You telling us he was a racist? A black guy who hated blacks?"

"Oh, he hated black women, for sure. Dated 'em, married one once, made 'em miserable. Monica did a number and a half on him. But that's not what I mean — he loved those kinds of complicated insults. You know, like 'mexcrement'. Wasn't that one of 'em? And spicaninny — that kinda stuff. Thought it was funny."

Skip thought back, hearing Clarke in her head: Polar bear, fish belly, flatass. He'd had a million of them.

"You know what? He probably even had a key to my

house. Look on his key chain. He used to take care of Bruno when I was gone. I never asked for it back."

And he knew the dog. So all he'd have to do would be to walk in, pet Bruno, and plant evidence, grabbing some more to take with him.

"But why would he do that?" Fazzio said. Skip could have sworn he actually looked hurt.

"Because he could," she said. He already knew they suspected Fazzio. She and A.A. figured he'd gone to Marda's that night for two reasons only: to kill Cody and frame Fazzio. Finding his phone would have been a bonus, but with Cody dead, it might never be found. He'd just miscalculated on how much time he'd need.

If he'd managed to kill Cody and strew his fake clues, they'd have found the second phone at Fazzio's — she had no doubt it had incriminating evidence on it — and that would have been that.

But she figured the real answer was as complex as any of Clarke's other motives — because the wall-writing had long pre-dated Cody's escape.

"Hey, Permy," Fazzio said as they were leaving. "The bitch moved out on me. So when are we gonna get together?"

Skip watched the self-possessed Read squirm before her eyes. "I don't date colleagues," she finally managed to stammer.

"More's the pity," Abasolo said.

As soon as they got the phone charged, they found what Clarke wanted them to find — pictures of the couple killed in Emily Martinez' house.

"What an asshole," Read said.

Skip agreed. "Yeah. Both of 'em."

24

Steve poured her a glass of champagne. "We've got a lot to celebrate! Miguel's dead, the whale's dead, and Cody's safe. Well done, Sergeant Langdon!"

"Ummm... thanks, but that happened almost two weeks ago."

He ignored her. "Boy, would I love to tell that kid's story!"

She gave him the evil eye. "Don't even think about it. The last thing she needs is more media hounding her."

He laughed. "You're so easy to bait, you know that? How about I just tell Sheba's instead?"

"Wait, what? I'm a little lost here."

"You know, the famous dog rescued from a serial killer..."

"That's not the part I'm confused about."

"I have news."

"Oho. Hence the champagne."

"I figured out a way I can work here. In New Orleans. And I don't even have to do film editing."

"Tell!" Skip raised her glass — and an eyebrow. This was huge.

"You know how there's this huge hunger out there for online video? The Internet eats it like popcorn."

She nodded. "Sure. But I don't see you as a YouTube star."

"Hey, did you forget? News outlets live and die on video. Well, CNN does these short documentaries..."

"Now you have my attention."

"So I pitched them Sheba. And they bit! They loved that, so next I pitched them How One City's Coping With The Scourge of AirBnBad, then Miguel's trafficking ring in Texas... they took it all. This could be a regular gig."

"Hmmm, good thing you have a cop for a girl friend. Or I can't think where you'd get your ideas." She got up to hug him.

"Damn good thing."

"It's funny you should mention Sheba. I had the most touching call today..."

CODY REALLY DIDN'T KNOW how she could have managed that first night without the dogs. As if they knew something was very wrong, they'd glued themselves to her even tighter than usual and somehow soothed her into slumber. She and Maw-Maw and Zachary had moved to a dog-friendly hotel, after a hysterical call with Mikey — hysterical on his part, mostly.

Maw-Maw assured him she'd get one of those crime scene cleaning services for Marda's house, but Cody doubted Mikey'd be invited to house-sit again. And she felt bad about that. But she shouldn't, her new therapist said.

Boo, her name was, and she'd been recommended by, of all people, Skip the cop. Boo lived right in the French Quarter. She was great pals with Mikey's friend Marda, and knew Marcia And The Band almost as well as Cody did.

Boo made Cody feel clean and whole again. Just being in her presence did that, never mind the rest of it, the part where Cody started crying almost the minute she walked in and hardly stopped at any time in the next hour. She had a lot to be sad about, Boo said, but a lot to be grateful for, not the least of which was that she'd finally found her home, after never having one with her own mom.

In fact an entire home was being created just for her.

Zachary and Maw-Maw were finally getting married. They were looking for a house to buy, having already moved out of their senior residence into a temporary (but dog-friendly) rental in New Orleans, where they wanted to stay while Cody was seeing Boo.

"I only moved to St. Anthony's because my kids didn't want me to be alone," Zachary explained. And Maw-Maw said, "I only moved there because he was there."

"So," Zachary continued, "now I'm not alone. I'm gonna have me a wife and a brand new granddaughter and a brand new house."

"Plus Marda," Cody answered, cuddling her new puppy, named to honor the woman who'd unwittingly given her shelter when she needed it. Marda was a prescription from Boo. "Nothing helps her as much as Rambla and those four little furballs," she told Maw-Maw. "I think she needs a puppy. Badly."

Maw-Maw wanted to get her a Cavalier like Rambla, but Cody wanted a very particular kind of dog, and she knew she'd find her at a shelter. She wanted a rescue, because she was one herself; a black dog because she'd heard they were less likely to find homes, and a mixed breed because— well, because of a feeling she couldn't understand, but it had to do with those awful things the whale had written on the wall. Boo called it "empathy," but to Cody it felt more like some kind of answer to the despair she felt when she thought about the kind of person who could even make up those words.

She wanted a female too, a kind of stand-in for herself — small, female, and homeless until she found someone to love her. Also, a stand-in for Sheba.

Boo told her Sheba's story the first time Cody saw her, and Cody latched onto it like a life raft. Sheba had survived — and so would Cody.

When she wasn't feeling sad and afraid, she felt so happy she could almost feel her own skin glow. But there was one thing she still wanted. Boo said she could get it, she was pretty sure.

For days Cody rehearsed what she was going to say. And finally she got up the courage to make the call, which she did from Boo's office. She talked fast so she wouldn't lose her nerve. "Sergeant Langdon... umm, Skip, this is Cody. My therapist thought you might be able to help. I was just wondering — is there any way I could meet Sheba? I just... want to see her. Maybe take a selfie with her."

She thought the cop hesitated, but maybe she was just trying to figure out how to do it. Finally she said, "Of course, baby. If Sheba's up to having visitors, I bet she'd love to see you."

"Also, I have someone for Rambla to meet."

THE END

WE GUARANTEE OUR BOOKS…
AND WE LISTEN TO OUR READERS

We'll give you your money back if you find as many as five errors. (That's five verified errors— punctuation or spelling that leaves no room for judgment calls or alternatives.) If you find more than five, we'll give you a dollar for every one you catch up to twenty. More than that and we reproof and remake the book. Email mittie.bbn@gmail.com and it shall be done!

A Respectful Request

We hope you enjoyed *Murder on Magazine* and wonder if you'd consider reviewing it on Amazon (http://amzn.to/1mO5NG4 .) The author would be most grateful.

ALSO BY JULIE SMITH

The Talba Wallis Series

LOUISIANA HOTSHOT

LOUISIANA BIGSHOT

LOUISIANA LAMENT

P.I. ON A HOT TIN ROOF

As well as:

BAD GIRL SCHOOL (Writing as Red Q. Arthur)

WRITE FREE: Forget the Rules, Liberate Your Creativity, and Write a Novel That Sparkles

NEW ORLEANS NOIR (ed.)

NEW ORLEANS NOIR: The Classics (ed.)

ABOUT THE AUTHOR

Julie Smith is a New Orleans writer and former reporter for the *San Francisco Chronicle* and the *Times-Picayune*. NEW ORLEANS MOURNING, her first novel featuring New Orleans cop Skip Langdon, won the Edgar Allan Poe Award for Best Novel, and she has since published nine more highly acclaimed books in the series, plus spun off a second New Orleans series featuring PI and poet Talba Wallis.

She is also the author of the Rebecca Schwartz series and the Paul Mcdonald series (as J. Paul Drew), and a YA novel, BAD GIRL SCHOOL (as Red Q. Arthur). In addition to her novels, she's written numerous essays and short stories and is the editor of NEW ORLEANS NOIR and NEW ORLEANS NOIR: THE CLASSICS.